Forbidden Fruit

Terrace VI

Forbidden Fruit

Purgatorio Towers #6

Curated by
Sarah L. Johnson & Robert Bose

Illustrated by
Aaron Bilawchuck

THE SEVENTH TERRACE

TERRACE VI: FORBIDDEN FRUIT
ISBN 13: 978-1-9992001-4-5
The Seventh Terrace First Trade Paperback Edition - 2021

The Seventh Terrace
www.the-seventh-terrace.com

*For the Hunger
- endless and insatiable -
hunger.*

FORBIDDEN FRUITS

WELCOME

GARY

Dear New Arrivals to Terrace VI, greetings and welcome!

By now you've found your cadence amidst the feasting and purging and everything else one might do in excess, twenty-five hours a day, three hundred and sixty-nine days a year.

As you're well aware, Purgatory has been locked down due to a pesky malignancy. The rubble is growing moss, Starbucks is limited to the unpopular latte flavors such as paprika and dill, Nihilist Arby's is drive-through only, and despite prodigious saltings, the poet pits are bubbling over with putrid pandemic cantos. Even our most malevolently extroverted residents have retreated to the Basement

Commons to suck up all our bandwidth streaming Factory Prime. The Factory itself operates, as it always has and always will, instantly showering us with goods both necessary and frivolous—so take comfort in that small favor.

While little has changed within the Towers, especially with the Sloths on Terrace IV (Brenda asks that you please, *please,* refrain from banging on the glass), we encourage your nonsensical hoarding—though if you can spare a shrimp for Terry, your acting Terrace VI representative, he'd greatly appreciate it.

I now come to the Tower business at hand: organizing the community cookbook fundraiser for the Glutton's improved feasting chamber, the grand Omnique Volatili. It's no secret that I abhor charity in all forms, so the fundraiser will proceed as a Crowdfunder campaign. Participation is mandatory.

Gary

President
Purgatory Towers Tenant's Association

OMNIQUE VOLATILI CROWDFUNDER

PURGATORIO TOWERS TENANT ASSOCIATION

The Campaign

The feasting chambers of Terrace VI have a long and storied history. Even the names invoke a quiver: The Grand Triclinium. The Vomitorium. The Tenebris Spatium. Each room, a legend. Each room, a window into an aspect of gluttony, consumption, and utter ruin.

As all compelling explorations eventually grow stale and deplorable, the time has come to for renewal, the time has come for vicissitude, the time has come for… remodelling.

As you have undoubtably heard, the chamber off the Erythraeae Terrae has been sealed for centuries due to ectoplasmic hagfish squatting (likely the source of the mucosal elevator infestation two years ago). Thankfully, the cosmic horror has now vacated the chamber, though damages are extensive.

We propose, through this cookbook fundraiser, to restore the Omnique Volatili to its primeval state complete with modern stainless steel and hardened ceramic decorative motifs.

The Epicureanomicon

Atonement has never been so delicious with this narrative feast for the soul that just can't get enough. Of anything. Featuring recipes for every occasion, from intimate humiliations by candlelight, to a crowd pleasing brunch fit for the most finicky of fiends. Such are the gustatory delights to be found in these pages you might almost—almost—forget that ripe golden pear, eternally out of reach.

Bonus Rewards

For each cauldron of flesh donated, a bonus story, written by one of the damned, will be released for required reading. Be warned.

THE EPICUREANOMICON CROWDFUNDER

561.25 Pounds pledged of 1000 Pounds
144 Backers

SUPPORT LEVELS

Faith

Pledge a Quarter Pound of Flesh

Rewards:

- Warm fuzzies - back it because you believe in it.

Support the project for no reward, except the knowledge you might see another dawn.

29 backers

The Digital Book

Pledge a Half Pound of Flesh

Rewards:

- One digital copy of the Epicureanomicon (your choice of infernal formats).

Estimated Delivery: June

14 backers

The Book

Pledge a Pound of Flesh (but 'no jot of blood', whatever the hell Shakespeare meant. Did anyone actually read The Merchant of Venice?)

Rewards:

- One physical copy of the Epicureanomicon. (Trade Paperback)

Estimated Delivery: June

33 backers

The Book + Goodies

Pledge Two Pounds of Flesh (enter as many times as you want, no purchase necessary)

Rewards:

- One physical copy of the Epicureanomicon. (Hardcover)
- One goodie bag. (obscene sticker, button, bookmark, and dishwasher-unsafe mug)

Estimated Delivery: June

32 backers

The Book + Goodies + Signed Art Print

Pledge Ten Pounds of Flesh (and it's not like you can't stand to lose a little pandemic pudge)

Rewards:
- One physical copy of the signed, limited edition Epicureanomicon. (Hardcover, one of fifty, signed by all contributors)
- One goodie bag. (obscene sticker, button, bookmark, and mug)
- One 8"x12" print of the cover signed by the Abominable Aaron.

Estimated Delivery: June

Limited: 35 left out of 50

The Works + Dinner with Terry

Pledge One Hundred Pounds of Flesh (or more, because you didn't realize once you start sourdough you can never really stop)

Rewards:
- One physical copy of the signed, limited edition Epicureanomicon. (Bound in the skin of your choice, signed by all contributors in blood)
- One goodie bag. (obscene sticker, button, bookmark, and mug)
- One 8"x12" print of the cover by the Abominable Aaron.
- One candlelight shrimp feast with Terry.

Estimated Delivery: June

Limited: 1 left out of 1

VOMITUS BACCHANALIUS

MIKE THORN

I held up my two finest neckties, aorta red and candy blue, and studied them side by side. I'd spent a fair amount of money on both, but I'd always had a certain distaste for neckties. Although they masqueraded as gross codes of high status, I believed they signified the servile, the restricted, the choked.

After some consideration, I decided to ditch the tie idea altogether. Tonight was the twentieth anniversary of Vomitus Bacchanalius, guaranteed to be a particularly rowdy event, and I intended to enjoy myself to the fullest. I no longer felt obliged to adhere to trite matters of decorum and propriety. As a decade-long VB member, I'd earned the right not to risk ruining a perfectly good tie. Leave it to the newbies to show up looking prim, proper, and pretty before things got gooey.

I finished buttoning my navy silk shirt while studying my two-day stubble in the bureau-top mirror, swept fingers through my salty-peppery locks, and exited the bedroom. My stomach pleaded audibly as I crossed the hall. I smiled and thought, *Don't worry, tummy. You'll be fit to bust before the night's through.* In accordance with VB policies, I'd spent the past month abstaining from sex, pornography, animal products, and intoxicants of all kinds.

It made the event's release that much better.

Kate opened the door, her face aglow with anticipation. Her sleek silk dress made me feel immediately self-conscious about my bachelor chic attire. Her partner Chuck swooped in behind her, looking beautiful in a Tom Ford tuxedo, and I felt doubly like an imposter.

I stepped into the spacious foyer, my shoes echoing off the white tile floor. The room was luminous with yellow chandelier light. Something by Bartók drifted in from the parlor, the volume turned low.

"Jonathan!" Kate and Chuck said, their smiles packed with meticulously cleaned teeth.

"Kate! Chuck!" I spread my arms, Lamborghini keys dangling from my left hand. "Am I the first to arrive?"

"First to arrive and always the last to leave," Chuck said, stepping around his partner to give me a paternal slug in the chest. "You hungry old dog, you."

I rubbed my palms together and offered the gorgeous couple a Luciferian grin. "Do we get a taste now, or do we wait?"

Kate tilted backward at the waist, gripping her stomach and cackling ceilingward.

"Oh, Jonny, you groveling boy," Chuck said, seizing the back of my head and pulling our faces close together. His smile was fixed, unmoving, like it was painted on. "You know damn well that we've got to wait for the others."

My stomach practically roared as I matched his lascivious stare. "Can we at least have a peek at what the Doloks have prepared?"

Chuck squeezed the back of my skull and chuckled; it sounded like a growl, gusting spearmint breath across my face. He turned to Kate, cocking an eyebrow. "What do you say, my love?" he asked her. "Do we butt in on the little ones and ask for a sneak preview? Or do we behave ourselves and wait for festivities to begin?"

Before Kate could answer, the doorbell rang. She whipped her head to the door, then returned her eyes to Chuck. She smiled and said, "Alright, fine. You two go ahead and take a look… but if I find out that either of you indulged in even the slightest nibble, you will suffer my wrath."

I stared into Chuck's icy eyes and suppressed the urge to exclaim with glee.

"Let's not waste any time, buddy." He clapped the back of my head, like a running-back hitting the quarterback's helmet after a team huddle. Then, with uncharacteristic elegance for a man his size, he strode across the foyer.

I followed him through the parlor, where elegant furniture and polished hardwood gleamed under sexy lighting. Bartók played on from an elaborate stereo system, whose towering speakers looked like they'd been manufactured by some alien race; but I knew very well that the only thing an alien race would be preparing here tonight was our feast.

I swallowed a mouthful of saliva as I trailed Chuck through the double oak doors at the end of the room. Upon entering the kitchen, my nostrils were greeted by nothing I would describe as appetizing. To the contrary, there was the unmistakable stench of something burning.

The kitchen was organized to maximum effect—two industrial steel ovens were stationed across the room, all stovetop burners hard at work. At least a dozen of the diminutive Doloks bustled around the space, some holding ladles, others brandishing cutting knives that looked comically large in their tiny, slender-fingered hands. Their grey bodies were all lanky, dexterous limbs, legs and arms that danced busily from football-sized abdomens. Black eyes gleamed from their small, oval heads, absent of orifices save the tiny holes that were their mouths and ears. At the end of the room, one Dolok wore a chef's hat atop his oblong head; in his right hand he held an iPad, presumably stocked up with recipes and administrative notes. His insectile eyes were ringed with fatigue-wrinkles, but focused. He shot looks around the room and gestured with his free hand, fingers twitching and flicking.

"Burning," Chuck said plainly, turning to me with a murderous smirk. "Burning," he repeated, striding toward the culprit oven, where an open pot belched dark clouds of smoke. A Dolok who looked tall for her species (from my vantage, I gauged her at about four foot two) skittered frantically to the pot of burning liquid. She stirred one pot with her stick-thin left arm while removing the spoiled batch with her right.

Chuck snatched the Dolok by the back of the neck and slung her across the tile floor. Her limbs fluttered, fingers splaying open to send stir-spoons flying; dollops of hot blue liquid sprayed from the pots and hissed on the walls and floor.

"You stupid fuck," Chuck said. He towered over the shocked Dolok, who was flat on her back, her tiny chest heaving and her black eyes expanding with fear. She raised her hands in the air, a universal gesture that said, *Please don't hurt me*. "You land on *our* planet seeking sanctuary and you treat us like this?" Chuck seethed. "You can't even be bothered to pay attention to the pots on the stove? Huh?"

The creature crab-walked a retreat on her weird, long limbs. Nearby Doloks cast worried glances over their slender shoulders, but not for long. Their body language told me they'd seen this scene play out before. I was not so quick to look away. I'd never seen my big, gregarious friend Chuck engage in anything more aggressive than a bit of good-natured horseplay. The rage inscribed on his contorted features was startling.

"Okay, I see how it is." Chuck's shoulders bobbed with anger-breath. "Someone needs some time to reflect."

He stomped across the kitchen, knocking over several Doloks in the process. One unfortunate creature was bustling across the room with a pot full of bubbling lagno and got caught between Chuck's massive, pistoning legs. The Dolok tilted and spilled backward, noodle-like fingers gripping the pot for dear life. Hot lagno spattered, soaking and burning the bodies of nearby hard-working creatures. They bristled, twitched, and jolted in quiet pain. This whole debacle was a bold reminder of why our society had ever claimed Doloks as its workers in the first place: not only could they prepare the orgasmic concoction that was lagno while also living off our vomited excess, but they were also a completely silent race.

Chuck advanced on the Dolok in the chef's hat and yanked the iPad away. He turned to me with a confusingly endearing smile and said, "We call this one Gordon. You know, like Gordon Ramsay. The head honcho." Then, without missing a beat, he turned back around and punched the creature's aubergine-sized head. Lifted off his feet, Gordon went limp, sailing several feet before landing on the tiles with a disconcertingly boneless *splat*. Chuck surveyed the creature's crumpled form and nodded, as if satisfied. "Okay, let's not burn any more of the lagno, yeah?" He clapped his big mitts together.

It was some weird performance, this pretense that the Doloks could understand our words. They'd long since been trained to comprehend our body language and the Vomitus Bacchanalius rituals, which all of us members always reassured each other (and ourselves) kept them happily employed.

Without us, they'd still be wandering near that shipwreck our ancestors discovered in the prairie all those decades ago. No shelter, no food, no nothing… it was a mutually beneficial relationship, and really, we were the ones helping them.

Convulsing, Gordon leaked bronze streams of blood from his tiny earholes.

It didn't take me long to shake off the shock. Soon enough, I was swishing top-tier Scotch inside my cheeks and surveying a roomful of exquisite faces and bodies, my stomach howling with expectation. A crystal chandelier and several vintage standing lamps washed the dozens of tuxedoed and gowned bodies with a golden glow. There were some familiar faces— mostly executives and presidents of national and international corporations—but also plenty of new ones; beaming young men and women with glittering smiles, wearing their salaries in the world's most prized designs.

Kate, reclining on a red chaise lounge while Chuck rubbed her shoulders, cast me a knowing smile from across the room. He must have told her about his kitchen meltdown. *It might've given you a start*, her expression said, *but it's necessary to keep those shits in line. And soon enough, you'll be so full of lagno you'll forget it ever happened.*

The noise in the room was escalating, voices emboldened by alcohol and arousal and hunger; the Bartók was now a nearly inaudible background distraction. Beside me, a man with a cul-de-sac of white hair ringing his whiter head said, "This is worth more than all the goddamn money in the world." The man beside him, face quivering beneath horn-rimmed glasses, nodded in agreement. The energy in the room seemed ready to reach its crescendo, eagerness building to almost violent heights. A woman standing beside the hearth twisted her husband's nipples through his button-down and cried out, "I could just *fuck* a bowl of that goop right now!"

Her squat hubby screamed in agonistic ecstasy.

As if cued, the kitchen doors burst open to reveal a line of Doloks in white uniform, their emaciated bodies no longer visible. The sight of their bare anatomies would be unsuitable for the eyes of this high society crowd.

Chuck raised a fizzing glass of champagne and cried, "Clear some space for our helpers, ladies and gentlemen! Back against the walls!"

The guests were already tightly packed—I estimated this to be the most well-attended VB event I'd ever seen—but with some careful shuffling, everyone cleared a path between the kitchen and the enormous banquet table. Shouldering bowls of lagno, the Doloks marched toward the table and began setting the dishes down, one by one.

A young man across the room turned to his handsome partner, kissed him on the lips and said, "This is it, Ronald. This is really it." Ronald smiled an affirmation of awe, his green eyes fixed on the servile creatures.

I found myself remembering my first VB event. Like Ronald and his woozy partner (and everyone else in this room, at some point), I had once been scintillated by that initial invitation, written in cryptic, alluring language that strictly mandated the utmost confidentiality.

The creatures moved with mute efficiency, covering the table with teeming bowls of lagno. Next, they formed two lines, half facing a crowd on each side of the room. They bowed as one, reassembled as a single column, and filed back into the kitchen.

"Y'see?" White Cul-De-Sac turned to his friend. "They love doin' what they do."

Nearby, a woman with dyed blonde hair wore a smile that pushed her features to their thresholds, her lips extending nearly to her ears. Her eyes watered as she graced the exiting Doloks with genteel applause.

Chuck approached the lagno table, wielding his champagne flute like a chalice of sacrificial blood. His huge face was aglow with reverent eagerness. The rest of the guests went quiet. Ronald whispered to his partner, "Is that *him*?" and received a placating swat on the forearm in response.

"We will do this in an orderly manner, as always," Chuck said. "Returning guests, you know the drill. To the uninitiated—welcome. I am pleased to see so many wonderfully eager new faces. The Doloks have prepared what is sure to be a spectacular batch of lagno, cultivated from their extraterrestrial harvest of limko. We will first welcome the returning guests alphabetically by surname to fill their bowls, which are located in the closet to my left. Once the returning guests are served, the new attendees will be welcomed to do the same. We will eat our first batches in unison, and that, my dearest of friends, is sure to set the night into motion. It's never long before the lagno takes effect." He smiled toothily. "Once you've eaten your fill, you'll feel a bit squeamish. The returnees know what I'm saying." Scattered laughter across the room. "When nausea sets in, please make your way to the kitchen, where our lovely Dolok friends will have set up the Vomitus. This is a large bowl, about the size of a generous wading pool. Please aim your bile into that basin, from which our Dolok friends will have their fill."

A man standing near the table cupped a hand around his mouth and bellowed, "Eat my barf, you puny retards!" His eyes bulged from his red face, scanning the surroundings for approval. A couple guests gasped in shock. Their admonishment was drowned out by waves of hysterical laughter.

"Gentlemen, ladies, please." Chuck raised a hand. "Restrain yourselves. The celebrations are only now about to begin. Before we dig in, though, I've got one more reminder: I accept online payment for Vomitus Bacchanalius through the web link provided on your invitations. Many of you have already paid me, and I want to take this chance to thank you again for that. If you would like to leave a tip in the form of cash or cheque before making your exit at the end of the evening, there is a large silver receptacle near the front door." He licked his lips, splashed some champagne down his throat. "Now, let the celebrations begin." He reached into his pocket, produced his iPhone, and cleared his throat before reading out the first name: "Adams, Jane."

A short woman in a mauve gown glided through the crowd, nodding at Chuck as she made her way to the bowls. She re-emerged, hands trembling, and filled the dish with a ladle's worth of blue lagno. Once she was positioned back among the guests, Chuck looked down at his phone and continued: "Arnold, Brian."

Midway through my first bowl, the lagno started working its magic. It always began the same way—unplaceable somatic sensation, a trembling that resonated in my abdomen's chartless regions. The bodies around me started waving, like high flags in the wind. Were the other guests disrobing yet? It was hard to say, because my vision was clouding. I never could remember my lagno-induced actions the next day—only that I almost always woke up undressed, my head resting on the sweat-sticky flesh of some stranger, my body hot and tense from over-exertion.

"You can't even *begin* to understand the things that lagno does to you, the things it does to the human body, so don't try," Kate had said to me after one of my earliest ceremonies, a particularly bawdy event. "You want to know what happened to you last night? You became a teardrop on the eyelash of God, that's what happened."

The room's golden light was now omnipresent, overbearing—it consumed the hordes of heaving and gasping bodies, most of which were by now probably conjoined in sexual acts beyond my incapacitated abilities to perceive. I was well on my way to shedding my identification as Jonathan, my body a nucleus of pure energy navigating space much stranger than sobriety misdirected me to believe.

"Oh fuck." My voice ebbed from my lipless lips to join the white luminescence of Bartók's compositions. Cosmic synaesthesia: a telltale sign that the lagno was taking effect.

The music was everywhere, leaking through my porous and immaterial body, gluing me to the rest of the undulating attendees. Though my cock was no longer shackled by the illusion of physical demarcation, I felt it throb, almost leap; it might have entered someone's body—a mouth, a vagina, an asshole, a fist, who knew? I heard selfless sounds of exaltation, and my bodiless body seemed to explode beyond its arbitrarily determined boundaries. Who, or what, had the right to say I was a body, even *had* a body? Lagno brought down the pasteboard masks of appearance, and once again I stared truth in its gloriously scary and entropic face.

"Thank you, Vomitus Bacchanalius," I said, or I thought I said, before reeling toward the portal that awaited beyond the sea of untethered selves. Even in the deepest throes of lagno-release, I knew how to find my way to the vomitus. It was time to puke, and then it would be time to eat some more.

The kitchen carried a different atmosphere. I perceived the clamoring and uneasy packs of Doloks, gray blots of unhuman matter on the peripheries of my trip-fucked vision. The vomitus presented itself as a glorious marble behemoth. I tilted over at the waist and retched. My guts jolted with violent release, and for a loopy moment I thought that maybe I was ejaculating yet again. Once finished, I backed away from the vomitus. The ashen blobs scuttled around the basin and began sucking with their pin-prick mouths.

These creatures had unthinkably efficient metabolic systems, and they were able to subsist off barely any food at all. After any given VB event, they could go nearly six months before Chuck had to feed them again.

Eat up, you sad suckers.

I turned to leave the room, but not before catching a glimpse of Gordon standing behind the bobbing, slurping crowd of his staff. A fearsome red bruise covered half of the being's face, like a faded tattoo. Despite the hyper-sensory affects of the lagno trip, I couldn't ignore the way his wide, unblinking eyes scanned my face. Some of his crew raised their dripping faces from the basin of puke and matched his eyeline. Their expressions were somehow imploring, even adversarial.

In a moment of clarity, I reminded myself that I was currently high beyond belief on weird liquid originally harvested on some unseen planet, and that I'd experienced similarly paranoid sensations while tripping on psilocybin and cannabis in my college years.

High as hell, that's all. You're just high as hell, and you're seeing things.

For no reason other than my own self-assurance, I smiled at the vomit-fed Doloks before exiting the kitchen. I stepped back into the parlour, abuzz with energy I can only describe as unharnessed stardust aphrodisia, and hunger descended. More lagno; that was what I needed.

I slipped through the rabble with my eyes set on the banquet table. All around me, bodies moved with acrobatically orgiastic movement. Moans seemed to rise in harmony, creating a new kind of symphony to accompany Bartók's concerto.

I arrived at the banquet table, and for a moment doubted my perception's accuracy. Not a single bowl of lagno remained.

Okay. It's okay, I told myself, a pathetic attempt at composure.

Riding my high while the early tendrils of withdrawal slithered into my cortex, I swiftly gave up on the attempt.

"Chuck?" I called. My heart thumped, thumped, thumped. I let the nervousness take hold and cried out, "Chuck! Where's the lagno? Where's the *fucking* lagno, Chuck?"

VB events depended on an endless supply of this intoxicating azure goo. The Doloks prepared yearlong to meet the requirements of their insatiable guests. Kate had once told me that coming down from a lagno high while still conscious felt how she imagined anesthesia-less surgery might feel: *The purest panic,* she'd told me. *The purest horror.*

"Chuck! The fuck?" The words spewed from my mouth like sloppy, amorphous globs. "The lagno? Chuck the fuck!"

Nearby, a doggy-styling couple chimed in, shouting in unison: "Fuck the Chuck!"

I should not have had the faculties to perceive their sexual position, nor to make out their words. Cracks were forming in my lagno trip, and fast. As the couple pumped and yelled, yelled and pumped, "Fuck the Chuck!", I began hearing other exclamations, seeing other coital sights that were appalling and arousing in equal measure. The entire purpose of lagno was to fully submerge oneself in another psychological realm, oblivious to the bacchanalia's grotesquerie. I was beginning to feel as if I was in the shower, or on the can, and that someone had busted into the bathroom unannounced.

I formed a hand-trumpet around my mouth, a doomed effort to make myself heard over the din. "Chuck! Oh please for the love of fuck, Chuck!"

From behind, an abrupt and hackle-raising scream. I whipped around to behold a nude woman tumbling through the kitchen doorway, hands clawing at her eyes. Gray-bluish liquid dripped from her face, steaming visibly in the parlor's opulent light. She went rigid and fell forward with a smack; I grimaced at the sound. She twitched and writhed, her hips bucking and her neck snapping side to side. Smothered by hardwood and goo, her mouth still managed to release loud cries of agony.

I made a move to approach her when another guest exploded from the kitchen: a young man, twenty-five at the oldest, donning nothing but an unbuttoned shirt. His face was a blob of hissing, off-colored ooze, his abdomen trickling and roiling with the same stuff. He twirled like a ketamine-doped ballerina and tilted sideways, his neck cracking to a ninety-degree angle as skull met wall.

These were not hallucinations. I was witnessing material reality, and it did not resemble what I'd ever expected to see at such a high society party. Sometimes our drugged-out pleasure elevated us to planes that approximated something like pain, but nobody was ever to sustain injuries at a VB event. I looked at the goo-faced man, whose unmoving body had landed beside two women lost in their own passionate embrace. *This is not simply a matter of injury*, I thought. *This poor bastard is dead.*

The rest happened fast, or maybe the remnants of lagno were sending my perception of time off-balance.

Gordon stamped out of the kitchen, gripping his chef's hat tightly in his right hand, his black eyes glaring. His Dolok staff filed behind him, their stomachs swollen with regurgitated slime.

Was I the only one sober enough to comprehend these goings-on? I whipped my head around the room. Bodies roiled in wild sexual permutations. The air was thick with the pungency of Iagno and sweat and fucking.

"Chuck? Anyone?" I sputtered. "Two guests have just fucking *croaked*, and the staff is leaving the kitchen! Nobody else is hankering for a refill yet? Nobody else is coming down?"

Gordon tilted his head. His inhuman eyes conveyed nothing.

I whirled around with every intention of splitting the scene, but there was no clear path to the door. The room was clogged with women and men in various states of undress, messed up on extraterrestrial drugs and profoundly enwrapped in crazed hypersexual union. Was this all Vomitus Bacchanalius represented? A chance for us super-wealthy fat cats to get high and cheat on our spouses without the distracting buggery of sober conscience?

Swarms of Doloks scuttled across the room to my right and left, vaulting over heaving mounds of bare, perspiring human skin. The creatures formed a circle around the room while Gordon stood, sentry-like, at the kitchen entrance.

It dawned on me with horrible, ludicrous clarity: they were preparing a firing squad. And I finally pinpointed Chuck on the other end of the room, oblivious to all reality on this terrestrial plane, his face buried between a woman's buttocks. He might as well have been in a different neighborhood, a different city, a different world.

I turned back toward Gordon, and I made the futile attempt to facially convey something like apology, or a plea for mercy. I dropped my eyebrows, slumped my shoulders and implored him with my watering eyes.

I knew his tiny mouth was incapable of such a thing, but I could have sworn he smiled. He held his arms aloft like a conductor leading his orchestra to the crescendo, bowed, and twitched.

There was a moment where the room seemed to tense like one giant organism, every guest's muscles squeezed tight in a breath between movement. It probably lasted a second or two at most, but it seemed to span the duration of a year. I cried out in terrible resignation, "Ohhhh," and then the mutinous beings let fly. They popped open their mouths and spewed geysers of regurgitated regurgitation all over the piles of humping and sucking and licking VB attendees. The bile hissed upon impact, reminding me of steak hitting a hot grill. The litany of moans changed tune, going quickly and horrifically out of sync with Bartók's incessant musical backdrop. The streams lasted an astonishingly long time—I cast my horrified gaze up the closest row of Doloks and saw their stomachs slowly retracting into their bodies, all their collective contents expelling in heavy and well-aimed synchronicity. The puke covered the crowds in a sheet and kept spilling over, trickling into mouths and nostrils, ear canals and eye-sockets.

I watched, paralyzed, as the rest of the guests submitted to this slaughter of Technicolor yawn. Their helpless bodies squirmed and thrashed and spasmed, like death-bound pigs squeezed into an industrial pen.

Revenge, I thought. *These Dolok creeps want revenge.*

I opened my mouth to scream, and then a weight slammed into the back of my head. Gordon's face dipped down into my vision as he latched onto me. He had ambushed me from behind, grabbing hold with his legs wrapped around my neck. He jammed his hands into my mouth, latching one set of fingers beneath my upper row of teeth, while his other hand yanked my bottom lip down toward my chin. I lurched forward, my foot meeting the lashing back of a barf-soaked man. I tried to bite down, but the little fucker was strong and persistent.

His weird, buggy eyes filled my vision as he lowered himself into position. Then his maw opened, and he sprayed a hot jet directly into my wide, gaping mouth. It sprayed my tongue, hit my uvula, coated the insides of my cheeks. It tasted like stomach acid. I choked and sputtered, but it was too late.

The effect was like the most potent dose of lagno amplified by a thousand, tilting far beyond the terrain of pleasure and into the domain of instant, insurmountable dread. My sense of physical self dropped away with the speed and violence of a gunshot; I hurtled down, down, down, flattened against the floorboards before being pulled into them, snagged among their tightly bound fibers, my vision abuzz with red-brown vessels that seemed to throb with frantic sentience. I spiralled past the fibers, going deeper, going smaller. I was a nonshape speeding amidst a disharmony of cells, which crackled with a dumb hungry *drive* for movement. The cells were swollen and ever-shifting globes that appeared to be comprised of infinite, tightly bound holes, and I wondered how anti-matter could constitute something that looked so horribly and convincingly solid. I sensed that I was now at the whims of a chaotic, relentless network that sought nothing but copula, baseless connection propagated only by a forceful and centreless *Will.* Sucked into the anti-cosmic shadow of a lagno high, melting into this substance's hellish underside.

The word *cosmos* implied order, arrangement, something of a system. Hurtling through this colorless and misshapen whorl, I saw nothing but the mayhem underlying the basis of this thing I called *the world*. Crackling spears of energy sprayed among these churning pools of anti-cells, sometimes connecting and sometimes splitting the cells in two. Indeed, I thought of plant roots and their probing, subterranean ambitions. I thought of stars done and undone, of eggs laid by species undiscovered by humans, and of the messy, animal imperative of sexual intercourse. I saw oceans of gametes and pistils, scores of sperm and fields of fertile ovum. I saw universes, and I knew that at the bottom it was all *this*.

I went deeper and darker and deeper and darker, and on some planet infinitely distant from here rang a chorus of silent laughs. Stoic Doloks cast their visions skyward, psychically perceiving my dissolution from the vantage of a strange planet whose ecosystems glowed bioluminescent purple. Their telepathic mirth was loud and indifferent, and I felt millions of their black eyes on my nonexistent face.

I would scream if I had a voice. I would scream if I existed.

The Dolok laughs accompanied me as I split through the ocean of cellular turmoil and into something that could not be described as something. The laughs were the soundtrack of my descent beyond the realm of space and matter; they were the demonic cacophony that ushered me out of this thing that my naïve human stupidity assured me was the real world. Somewhere in my absence, the I that I used to be was laughing, too. These sounds pulled me through the blackness of dwindling substance, drew me into the non-blackness of absolute negativity, and they sounded like music.

They sounded like Bartók.

PRODUCTION
UPDATE #1

 **Terry (coordinator)**
June 20th, 2021

Penguins will fuck anything. Including sharks. Especially sharks. Look, I have nothing against our illustrious President. What Gary does to rotting heads on sticks in his penthouse suite on Terrace VII is none of my bloody business, but now he's chummed the water and left me in charge of this wretched cookbook.

First, the good news. Thanks to your generous compulsory backing, we are fully funded! The bad news, obviously, is that we are a little behind, but we're gathering recipes, and barring any more unnatural acts of Gary, expect to be back on track very soon!

THE ACCIDENTAL DOMINATRIX

SARAH L. JOHNSON

When we split, you took everything – the plants, the furniture, the blender, even the damn light bulbs – like a hot little grinch in yoga pants. And I let you because I'm a fucking doormat. Except for the Vitamix, I don't think you wanted any of that shit, you just kept taking stuff to see where I'd draw the line, and I never did. Setting boundaries isn't my strong suit. I'm lazy, and it's easier to be pushed than to push back. I've never found much in life to be worth the effort. I guess not even you. In the end you left me with the one thing neither of us wanted.

Lazlo.

Inherited from your grandfather – dead two weeks before anyone checked on him – the cat came to us in rough shape, a mangy strip of gristle with hell for a personality. He didn't exactly take to you, but fuck did he hate me. I couldn't walk through a room without that thing hissing from some dark corner. Couldn't take a nap on the couch without feeling its muddy green eyes glaring death in my direction. Hardly ever would I catch it out in the open, rather it existed as an ugly flash in my periphery, a puff of dirty fur, the sharp angle of a skinny leg, the grating *tick tick tick* of its ragged claws on the hardwood. Or the nasty smacking as he gummed down his vegan kibble with broken teeth. Whoever heard of a vegan cat? Explains a lot, actually.

And I know you already know all of this, I just want *you* to know that *I* know, so you don't think I'm fabricating. One thing you may not know is that I did what any heartbroken dude would do after being dumped. I ate garbage, neglected my hygiene, and got blackout drunk in the same pair of sweats every day. And finally, in the grip of a raspberry Sourpuss bender, I reached out for help.

Tick tick tick

Tick tick tick

Tick tick tick

I groaned as a rumble drilled into my ribcage, shattering the one respite I had from my sad shit-swamp of a life. Morning already? Was the garbage truck here? A definite smell wafted in. I flinched at a flurry of sharp pokes into my chest like an angry acupuncturist.

"Ow, ow, ow!" I gasped opening my eyes, and swatting at the cat. With a muddy glare and bristle of his few remaining whiskers, he shambled out of the bathroom, probably to hide under his favourite ottoman like a goblin. I rubbed my t-shirt over the burning claw marks. "Goddamnit, Lazlo, what the hell?"

My crimped spine protested as I hoisted myself off the tiles and looked in the mirror. Hair sticking up in greasy chunks, hangover stink, same filthy sweats. A hot-ass mess. I grabbed my phone to check the time and found it open to the online marketplace where I'd apparently been browsing in the deeply cheap furniture section before blacking out.

God your cat sucks. Seriously.

I burped a caustic cloud of raspberry, reminding me of your birthday when I was pouring Sourpuss shooters for you and your girlfriends and I held your hair back while you puked up red foam and thought you were dying.

I'd been drinking my way through the dregs of our liquor cabinet. You'd loved those boozy confections, and each bottle was a memory. I guess you were okay with me keeping those.

My phone buzzed with a text.

Blair: Hey, I'm coming over to grab a few more things.

My heart tumbled. You were coming over. Again. Maybe for the last time. I wondered what else you wanted from me. Wondered what I had left. Maybe you'd finally take the cat. The doorbell echoed through the newly hollow bungalow.

I peered at the mirror through blood-webbed eyes and scraped my fingers through my hair. Wow, worse. Pit sniff, oh god… I ran down the hall, taking in the domestic Armageddon all around me. Pizza boxes, Chinese takeout, tetrapaks of Palm Bay, and so many flavoured vodka bottles: mini marshmallow, birthday cake, cinnamon swirl. Dirty socks, dirty dishes, and kitty litter tracked fucking everywhere. At least the foul thing used his box. Which was about all I could claim as well. Christ, we deserved each other. I cracked the kitchen window to vent the despair. The doorbell rang again, and I hung my head. This was it.

"Did you forget your key—Jesus!" I jumped back from the open door.

It's not every day someone in a full gimp suit shows up on your porch, so forgive me for not knowing exactly what to do. And I know what you're thinking. Standard kit: shiny black PVC deal, with buckles, grommets, and zips. The kind of American Horror Story get up you see when you accidentally click instead of closing popups on Pornhub.

And it was that, but also not.

The suit covered them head to toe, but the mask didn't have any eye or nose holes, just a chunky steel zipper stretching across the bottom half of their face like a too-long smile. I wasn't sure how they could breathe, unless there was some hidden panel or mesh or something I couldn't see – which was possible because the other thing about the suit, was that you couldn't really see it at all. It wasn't shiny, rather a totally matte black. Not just black, something more than black. So dark and featureless it burned away all the light around it, blurring the edges in a way that the longer I stared, the more it expanded, the more I leaned into its gravity, ready to fall into that blackness, into a deep, empty nothing.

Have you ever gone along with something you knew you shouldn't? Latched onto some detail to rationalize the situation, because to do otherwise is somehow too onerous or embarrassing? Like you're the one that's weird or rude for pointing out the purple leprechaun? Actually, I bet not. You're good at setting boundaries. This wouldn't have happened to you.

For the record, I totally would have slammed the door in the gimp's face and called 911 if not for the weirdest thing of all: the mop and bucket at their side. That's what gave this fucked up scenario enough credibility that I felt I at least owed the stranger decked out in full fetish gear standing on my porch on a Sunday morning a chance to explain. Maybe it was a joke. Maybe they were some little league team's mascot. What did I know? I can't say I was thinking clearly. It was the suit. That weird black suit. Like that blackness had reached into me, touched something, and made me want more.

"Can..." I pressed my eyes closed and swallowed a sour mouthful of saliva down my dry throat. "Can I help you?"

The gimp held up the mop.

I shrugged. "Yeah, I don't..."

A breeze ruffled the leaves of my laurel tree and sparrows sang good morning songs to one another. The gimp leaned the mop against the porch rail, stooped to pull a phone out of the bucket, and showed me the screen.

A browser page open to an ad on the same marketplace I frequented. An ad I had apparently placed at 3 a.m.

Wanted: Domestic servant for Mean Kitty
Description: Pet duties and housekeeping
Compensation: Lifetime supply of vegan kibble
Contact: Ashley

A mossy memory surfaced, of giggling, glass of Sourpuss clamped between my teeth, taking a break from surfing eight-dollar couches to thumb out my own death sentence and post it in the personal ads. I could see why they might think...I opened my email and sure enough, there it was, the confirmation at 3:08, and a reply at 3:12.

Dear Madam,
I am extremely interested in the position. Experienced in both pet play, SSC and RACK rules, and can provide my own equipment.
It would be an honour to serve you.
Yours,
V

"The fuck..." I muttered to myself. "I'm sorry this is a mistake..." I trailed off when I saw I'd replied to them, with my home address and the invitation to *come over any time*.

Well, they had. And they weren't running away, though clearly I was no *Madam*. My phone dinged. You, of course.

Blair: Running late. Be there in an hour?

"Shit," I said, looking over my shoulder and shuddering. You'd be walking into Beirut, removing all doubt that you'd dodged not just a bullet, but a cannon. I looked back at the gimp. At the mop and bucket. "You really wanna clean my house?"

They didn't speak, or nod, or move at all.

"Can you do it in an hour?"

Nothing but a slight bow of their head. They were hardcore. And it hit me: I was playing the game wrong, rather I wasn't playing at all. I wanted something from them, but they expected something too. First thing they probably expected was for me to be a woman. A whip wielding dominatrix ready to grind her stilettos into their balls – if they had any. I could at least try to play along.

"So…you're gonna come in," I said, my voice rasping, then closing around the syllables with authority. "You're gonna come in and clean my house and it better be done in an hour."

Another slight head tilt, I couldn't be sure because looking at that blurry black made my stomach shiver. "Nod if you understand."

They nodded.

I stepped aside. "Consider this your audition. Get to work."

V. Their name was V, and they moved with surprising grace for a pervert. They wore that suit like Spiderman, the kind of body that made me extremely aware of the weight I'd accumulated over the last couple years with you. The insidious pudge you put on when you're too happy to give a fuck about what eating Korean noodles at midnight is doing to your metabolism. Not that you ever seemed to gain an ounce. Again, boundaries. Plus all that pranayama. God, I miss your yoga butt.

I watched V for a while, picking up trash and loading it into bags. Piling dirty socks into a laundry basket. Wiping down tables and shelves. Methodical. Thorough. But too slow.

"Hey, can you maybe…?" I paused, remembering my role, even though I had no idea what the hell I was doing, or what SSC or RACK stood for. "Hurry it up. I've got company in half an hour."

That blurry ass suit couldn't hide their shudder, or their pleasure. Reacting to my voice, to my authority. "I'm gonna have a shower and by the time I'm out, I want this done."

V nodded.

The perfect opportunity for murder, or at least robbery. I considered it a test of our fifteen-minute relationship. If you don't have trust, what do you have? And the one thing V couldn't clean was me. When I got out of the shower, I found the house not totally spotless – they weren't Mary fucking Poppins – but it no longer resembled an episode of Intervention. And it smelled…well, it didn't smell.

V sat on the couch, back to me, and I heard a sound, low and somehow wet, like a clogged meat grinder. Lazlo sat in V's lap, swaddled in a black void, purring, as they ran the pet brush through his matted fur. The cat cracked open eyes the color of duck slime and glared.

"You gotta go. Now." I shoved the cat, who awkwardly thumped onto the floor and scuttled under his ottoman, likely to swipe at my ankles the next time I walked by.

V didn't move. Okay, fine, part of the game. "Get up."

Panic pricked the soles of my feet. If you walked in and saw this? Yeah, dunzo. I gripped V's wrist hard enough that I should have felt the press of bones but felt only the spongy black of the suit. I didn't like touching it. I objected to it.

It offended me. This was my house and I wanted this filthy weirdo gone.

"Get out now," I yanked the gimp's arm and with a petty show of resistance they rose from the couch, head hung low, but that zipper set in a permanently stretched out smirk. They collected their supplies and plodded to the door where they paused, rubbing their wrist. My booze bloated guts cramped in shame. "Jesus, I'm sorry."

They shook their head and took my hand between their loathsome gloves, bringing it to their cheek, nuzzling it like a kitten. The suit grazed the back of my knuckles like rubber and velvet at the same time. I pulled my hand back, wiping it on my jeans. V picked up their mop and bucket and left.

I didn't watch them go, didn't want to see them take off the mask and get into a blue Hyundai. I didn't want to see which direction they drove off in. Like a lot of things in life. At least my life. Sometimes you're better off not knowing where a thing comes from. Especially if you want more of it.

In the kitchen, I pulled a pack of coffee beans from the freezer. Some ethical artisanal crap you paid fifty bucks a pound for. The grinder made its racket and the roasted aroma filled the air as I tried to reconcile what happened, and convince myself I hadn't liked it. Not even a little. Not even at all.

"Smells good in here!"

I nearly knocked the fresh grounds off the counter. "Oh, hey."

You wrinkled your nose in the way that lifts your top lip slightly and makes you look like a rabbit. Purple leggings paired nicely with the vintage Back to the Future t-shirt you stole from me when you moved out.

"Place looks..." You surveyed the notable lack of trash and disorder.

"Work in progress," I said, pouring water into the coffee maker and starting the brew. "Been meaning to Kondo the place."

"Really?" You gave me a skeptical look, toes curling into your flip flops.

"Really. Like who needs a shower curtain?"

"Yeah, sorry, it's just...well, you know my grandma gave me that shower curtain. And if it's okay, I thought I'd take the TV?"

"The TV?" I poured coffee into two mugs, handing her one. "Blair...I bought that before we moved in together."

"You only watch stuff on your iPad, and I can't afford one right now with getting my own place set up."

"Right, for sure," I said, burning my mouth on the metallic sludge and swallowing anyway because I have a bottomless appetite for pain and you'd faint if I defiled your good coffee with dairy. "So, how have you been?"

We chatted and chirped at one another in the too-friendly way of exes in limbo. You talked about your promotion to the design team, the omg so much shorter commute from your new place to the office, your parents being dramatic over the breakup, and if I'm being honest, I realized something that morning. In spite of your yogi lifestyle, cool job, hot ass, and arty friends…you're not very interesting. And I still missed you so much it made my bones ache.

"They like you, I get it, but you'd think they'd want me to do what's right for me, and not settle," you said, and in one derisive snort drove a fork through my aorta without even realizing it. You squeezed my hand. "Want to help me pack a few things?"

I squeezed back. "Sure."

Putting on your favourite playlist of ukulele covers, I helped you pack your organic cotton tote bags full of towels, the toothbrush holder, my favourite mug before I could even finish my coffee, and all the cutlery but a single setting because, "C'mon, Ash. All you eat is sandwiches and takeout."

"True." I slid the emptied drawer shut. "Are you hungry?"

We ordered donairs because you'd decided you weren't vegetarian that day and ate them on the couch while Lazlo watched like a creep from under the ottoman.

"Hey buddy," you said, flicking a shred of beef onto the freshly mopped floor. The cat slithered forward, sniffed at the morsel and gagged.

"He's vegan, Blair."

"Right, I forgot." You pulled a face. "He looks…did you give him a bath or something?"

I wasn't sure what to say, or not say, so I shrugged. "You going to take him?"

You bit your lip, the way you always do when you want people to think you feel bad. "Could you keep him a little longer, just until I get settled."

"No problem," I lied, setting my half-eaten sandwich on the coffee table. "Take as much time as you need."

I was pulling the entertainment center back to unplug everything when you stared at the pile of tote bags, plus the two kitchen chairs you'd decided to take, because apparently I never ate in the kitchen anyway.

"This is going to fill up the car," you said. "Could I come back later this week for the TV?"

You'll probably laugh, but my heart blew up at the idea of seeing you again. More time. Could you be stalling? It never occurred to me. That's why you'd left the cat. That was all I needed. More time. And there you were, handing it to me. "Wednesday? We could do this again, have dinner."

"Cool," you said with one of your easy smiles as you slipped on your jacket. "I'm glad we can still hang out. I've missed it."

"Yeah," I watched your toes wriggle back into those grungy flipflops. I missed your toes, and your leggings inside out all over the bedroom floor, and your tiny tits, Jesus… "Me too."

We loaded your car with my stuff, and you drove away. You never did tell me where your new place was. I never did ask. Remember what I said about not knowing? Thinking about your new apartment gave our situation an unpleasant tangibility, like sinking your hands into memory foam, the way it creeps into all the empty spaces until you can't move.

I floated back into my home, with its bare walls and empty shelves, a house slowly decanted of its wares. You were coming back. I'd told you to come over and you were going to. I told the gimp to clean and they did. I gave orders, and they were obeyed. I sucked in a breath I didn't realize I'd been denying myself and the air filled a space inside me I didn't know I'd had, like an opening void.

Much like the house, however, my act wasn't an overnight clean up. I needed a drink. Rifling through the cupboard, my options were limited to more Sourpuss – god no – or a dusty bottle of Midori. I retrieved one of two tumblers left in my custody and poured a couple fingers of green liqueur. The melon stench burnt my nose before the first drops reached my tongue. Maybe I'd buy a nice bottle of wine for Wednesday. You'd like that. Over the rim of the tumbler, I caught a flash of patchy fur. Without thinking I winged the glass at the wall. It shattered, showering the hardwood in glass and glittering green rain. The cat yowled and scurried down the dark hallway.

After a moment of deliberation, I tugged my phone from my pocket and typed out an email.

V,
Congratulations, you've got the job. Come back tomorrow and finish it.
Ash

A reply came within a minute.

Dear Madam,
I'd be honoured.
V

By morning all my swagger had seeped between the floorboards like the Midori. When the doorbell rang, I turned the knob with a sweaty hand. Right, so I hadn't imagined it. Same matte black dimming the world around it. Same too-wide zipper smile in an eyeless mask, taking in the sticky puddle of melon liqueur and broken glass behind me.

"Please, come in," I said before I remembered my job, to be in command. I could do that. I could make the rules. And that was important. Rules. Boundaries. I'd stayed up most of the night researching in preparation. "Sit down, we need to discuss some things before we begin today."

V nodded, heading directly for the couch, though pausing to pet Lazlo's scabby little head as the cat ground out his rusty purr and twined around their darkness clad legs.

"Sit," I snapped, resisting the urge to immediately apologize when they nodded meekly.

"Okay...V." I perched on the couch, and rolled with it when instead of sitting next to me they knelt at my feet. I kept my gaze on my hands. "First of all, I'm very happy with the work you did yesterday."

They leaned in resting their cheek against my knee, the edge of the zipper scraping against my jeans even as the cat rubbed his face against the hypnotic black suit.

"Right, uh…first, this isn't a sexual thing for me, no judgment or anything, it's just not. So, I'm not going to touch you that way. And I won't ask you to touch me either, okay?"

A nod. I couldn't tell if it was disappointment, relief or indifference, but they kept their cheek resting on my knee and I found I liked the weight.

"The other thing is I'm new to this, so I can give orders and push you around and stuff but I need to know what your limits are."

V's head lifted and swiveled side to side.

"You don't have any?"

Another shake.

"Obviously I don't want to actually hurt you."

Another shake, but one that seemed condescending, which annoyed me.

"At the very least we need a safe word." I kicked the cat away, still purring and nuzzling V, who was more rightly my pet than the cat. "How about Lazlo? If it goes too far, or you want me to stop for any reason, you say Lazlo."

A nod.

"Can you say it, so I know you understand?"

They didn't say it. I didn't push. And in this way, we came to an agreement, because the moment he said the safe word would be the moment it ended. Forever.

Stupid, I know. But like I said, it doesn't take much to rationalize going along with something you absolutely should not go along with. You would have noped on outta there, but you have to remember, I was only beginning to learn how to do that.

"Fine." I planted a foot in the center of their chest and shoved. "Get to work in the kitchen. Feed the cat, too. His food smells like shit, so good thing you're wearing that mask."

V gathered the cat and headed for the kitchen in that oddly graceful glide. I couldn't help wondering what their body looked like underneath that sheath of darkness, what they felt like. I'd promised not to touch, not that way, but I found myself wanting to sink my fingers into the velvet black of that suit, harder and harder, until I got something, anything, out of them. Even just a gasp.

After a night glued to the screen, reading up on consent, risk awareness, hard and soft limits, aftercare, and falling down a terrifying rabbit hole or three, a nap would have been perfect. But no way could I sleep with a mute pervert swiffering all around. Finally, V neatly set their equipment by the door and bowed their head as I made a show of wandering room to room, inspecting the level of lemon-scented cleanliness I felt unqualified to assess. The sparkle in the bathroom nearly blinded me but I noticed a streak across the mirror. So obvious it had to be intentional. A question. A challenge. Would I hold up my end of the bargain?

With measured strides, I made my way to the front door and grabbed V by the scruff of their suit. They allowed me to manhandle them back to the bathroom and I pointed out the streaky mirror. "Does that look clean?"

They hung limp in my grip.

I forced their head closer to the mirror. "Answer me."

Could they even see? I squinted, trying to spot any slits in the mask for eyes, there must have been, but I couldn't see anything. When I stared at the suit, I couldn't see at all.

"Lick it clean," I whispered. V stiffened under my hand. Face and reflection collided in black blur, and with my other hand I pinched the tab of zipper stretching across his face like cruel steel stitches. I expected the tab to be warm, body temperature, but it was cold.

V's black glove slapped my hand away.

I stepped back, the sting in my knuckles pulsing in hot waves. What the hell? Was the zipper a hard limit? They said they didn't have any. I put myself out there to give them what they wanted and now they weren't doing it? Weird as it sounds, I was embarrassed. And then I was pissed. And I swung my arm across and whipped it back, cracking my hand across their face, metallic smirk shredding the skin of my offended knuckles.

"I said lick it." I wrapped both hands around their neck, resisting the urge to recoil when I didn't feel...well, anything. The structures of the neck, the muscle, cartilage, and vertebrae, it's like they weren't there. The suit had only the spongey bit of give of some defiant non-Newtonian fluid.

I slapped their face against the mirror. The zipper screeched against the glass and once again my fingers found the cold tab. V's wriggling abruptly stopped.

I pulled the tab back, one, two, three teeth. A sharp whiff of ozone blasted my sinuses. Darkness filled my vision and bile rushed up my throat. A sense of weightlessness and being swallowed obliterated my senses. Until I felt V's arms, catching me.

They hauled me out of the bathroom and draped me across the familiar terrain of our bed, and I closed my eyes inhaling the last traces of dry shampoo left in your pillowcase. All the sleep I didn't get the night before barreled down and I sensed V crawling around the bed and curling up on the floor on my side of the mattress. The cat purred and I rolled, flinging my arm over the edge, fingertips resting on the slick suit as I slipped into a yawning darkness.

And I didn't hate it.

The risotto burnt so bad I had to throw out the pot, leaving me with only a small egg pan. No good for impressing the woman I loved, so I ordered the expensive sushi and hoped the stench of burnt rice would air out in time. The sushi arrived fifteen minutes before you, so I opened the fridge and nearly had a heart attack when the harsh wedge of light illuminated the cat sitting in the middle of the kitchen.

"Shit," I muttered, and scooped a veggie roll out of the tray before shoving the rest in and closing the door. "C'mon, Laz. We gotta talk."

I set the roll in his food dish and carried it into the living room. The cat perched on the arm of the couch and I set the bowl in front of him. He dove in, making hideous smacking sounds as he devoured the three-dollar roll. I ran my palm down the emaciated mountain range of his spine. He whipped his head around and snarled.

"Jesus, okay," I said, withdrawing my hand, knuckles scabbed over from my altercation with V. I'd woken up alone that night, with my hand neatly bandaged and the cat glaring green hatred at me for driving away the only other creature he could tolerate. "Look, I know you're not happy."

The cat resumed gumming away at his expensive vegan meal. I realized I was rubbing the hand that touched the cat against the couch cushion as if attempting to scrape off something nasty.

"If Blair was going to take you, she would have done it by now, and I know the only person you like less than her is me. But you seem to like V a lot, don't you?"

Anyone who tells you cats can't understand humans is woefully ignorant. That animal didn't just look at me, he looked into me. Those murky eyes saw something, or nothing, and I didn't know which was worse.

"I haven't mentioned it yet," I said. "But if they agreed…would that make you happy? Going to live with them?"

Lazlo blinked slowly and then, like an asshole, pushed his bowl with the remains of his expensive dinner, off the edge of the couch. The dish clattered to the floor and the cat limped off to hide in some dark corner as I heard your key in the lock.

And that's when it all went to shit, if you really want to know. I just didn't realize it until later. You remember what happened though. After a few pleasantries I took care of business and loaded the TV into your car because I didn't want to make it awkward by making you ask. After that, the Sushi went over well, the wine even better.

"You hate rosé." You held out your glass for me to tip in the last of the bottle.

"I don't hate it. I just never thought much about it. This one is pretty good."

You scanned the room, slowly. "Seriously, did you get a housekeeper?"

Letting the last of my indeed very good rosé slide down my throat I nodded. "I may have called in some help." I glanced at Lazlo, scowling from under the ottoman.

You pillowed your head on my shoulder. "Remember when we moved in? Looked a lot like this."

"Clean?"

"Empty." You stretched your Lulu Lemon legs over the bare floor. "That first night, we were sitting right here, just like this."

"Pizza."

"And wine coolers, ugh." You laughed and clapped a hand over your face, smothering a snort.

I laughed with you. Really laughed, like I hadn't in so long it felt totally new, the warm tremble of your body pressed to mine.

"We were so happy to be out of that shit apartment," I said.

"We were so happy." You set the glass down, turning your face up to mine.

Here's something weird.

I couldn't remember the last time I'd kissed you. Probably I'd kissed you all the time, but I really couldn't remember, and that's what happens when you're with someone for a long time. You stop recording moments and it all shimmers into a homogenized history of Us. My body remembered though. My mouth remembered yours. I remembered how you smelled up close, everything the pillowcase couldn't hold, that briny funk of tea tree oil, dirty hair, and hot yoga.

"That night," you whispered, biting the rim of my ear. "Right here, on the floor. I had skinned knees."

"Amazing what you don't feel after three Bacardi Breezers—" I gasped as you slid your hand into my jeans, cold little fingers gripping me with more force than I remembered. "Jesus, Blair...are you sure?"

"I miss you." You stroked me as I spidered under your sweatshirt, finding your perfect braless nipples. "But if you don't want to..."

We managed to get two thirds of our clothes off and lost more than a little skin to the hardwood. The best sex we'd ever had because this is what you may not know: I didn't remember the night we moved in being that special. We'd never connected like this before. I felt your heartbeat all through your body, and when you came your eyes never left mine.

After, we curled up in a nest of our discarded clothes and you little spooned into me, sighing. "I love you, Ash."

I pushed my face into your hair and inhaled the unwashed film. "I love you."

We dozed on a cloud of sushi and pink wine. I roused only when I heard the sound of Lazlo licking the remains of sushi from the plates. I sat up, shooing him away. "Goddamn cat."

You stirred and yawned. "So much for being vegan."

"Let me put these plates away, then we can go to bed."

"Actually," you tugged your leggings up over your bare ass, "let me get something from the car."

"What?"

"You'll see," you said, kissing me. "But I think you'll like it."

You dashed out the door with your keys and I couldn't stop the grin from spreading on my face. Not that I cared about the damn TV, but it was symbolic. A miracle. Like I'd fucked some

Christmas spirit into the Grinch. Your heart grew three sizes and you were going to bring it back. All of it. Including yourself.

They say if you love someone, you have to let them go. I'd always thought someone who loved you wouldn't leave in the first place, let alone take all your stuff with them, but I'd never been so happy to be wrong.

Then you returned, not with the TV, but with a cat carrier. "Surprise!"

Did I say something? All I remember is the tinnitus, and the gutful of rosé threatening to reverse its trajectory. And believe me I enjoy telling you this about as much as you enjoy hearing it, but this is where we're at, and it won't be long now.

"He's my cat," you said. "It wasn't fair of me to leave him."

I shook my head. "I thought…"

Your caramel eyes followed my gaze to the floor where I'd been inside you not twenty minutes ago. "Oh…Ash, that's not what this is."

"Then why say…you love me?" My voice shriveled in my throat. "That you miss me?"

"Because I do!" you protested, somehow lying and showing me the most nakedly honest version of yourself all at once. You set the carrier down and opened its steel door. "But that's not enough to make it work. We tried."

"How can it not be enough? I gave you everything, Blair. What more do you want?"

"It's not just about what I want."

"All I ever needed was you."

Your mouth softened as though you wished things were different, and for what it's worth, I believed you. I still do.

"I can't be the only thing you want, Ash. I can't be that for anyone. It's like living with this emptiness that can't ever be filled. You're always so damn hungry. You need something, but it can't be me. I can't give that much of myself, to anyone. I'm so sorry."

Lazlo sauntered back into the living room, casually, like he hadn't been hiding his movements from us every day for years. You crouched. "Time to go, kitty. See your new home."

The cat sniffed in your direction and slunk away under the ottoman.

"Damn thing." You looked up. "Can you help me please?"

I went to stuff my hands in my pockets, forgetting I was just in my underwear. That's when I made up my mind. "No."

"Fine, whatever," you crawled towards the ottoman. The cat growled, as if warning off a snake slithering through the grass.

"I mean no, Blair. You can't take him."

You popped up, hands on your hips. "I don't need your permission."

"He hates you."

"He hates you too."

"I've got a new home for him."

"You were going to give away my cat?" Your voice rose an octave.

"Are you serious? You left me, took everything with you, including the goddamned kitchen chairs, and then you come over tonight to stir up all kinds of shit like you didn't break my fucking heart?"

You gazed up at me through your eyelashes. "This has been hard for me too."

"Get out."

"Ash..."

"Get the hell out." I opened the door as you gathered your things. "And Blair, don't come back."

Surely I get credit for not slamming that door, right? Because I closed it soft as a butterfly kiss, went back to the living room, and sprawled face down on the floor. From under the ottoman, Lazlo blinked slowly. I blinked back. He tucked his ugly skull under his paws and pretended to go to sleep.

Was I really that needy? *Hungry.* That was the word you used. *Empty.*

The doorbell rang.

"Whatever you left behind you can live without," I yelled. "We're done."

The doorbell rang again and I scanned the living room, spotting your pink thong, half tucked under the ottoman. Lazlo took a swipe at my wounded hand as I snatched them up and stomped to the door. "If you think…"

I dropped the panties.

V stood in that meek but expectant posture. Through the mask they must have somehow seen how totally wrecked I was because they stepped forward, gloved hands cradling my face and folding me into their arms. I flattened my hands against their back, pads of my fingers sinking into the foamy black suit. If I kept pressing I would sink right into them. That strange dizziness swamped me again and I staggered back.

"Fucking Christ, where do you even come from?"

Lazlo scampered gracelessly from under the damn ottoman to mew and slither around V's ankles.

"Hey, you want a cat? He seems to like you and I've got a lifetime supply of vegan kibble to throw in."

V shook their head.

"You don't want him?"

Silence.

"Can you please goddamn talk?"

They just stood there like a mute spiderman from hell. Then they knelt at my feet, face pressed against my naked legs, hands clutching the backs of my knees. Neither cold nor heat leached through the material of the suit, only that yielding darkness. But I wasn't done being mad. I kicked, hard enough that they fell back, shivering with pleasure. I felt a tingle myself. This was the role, though I wasn't sure we were playing.

"How am I the needy one?" I gave them another rough shove with my knee. "When she constantly shows up here taking from me?"

V shuddered. I yanked them to their feet. They were lighter than they should've been, or just more agile. "Still have nothing to say?" I shook them until their head rocked back and forth. "You like this? Being pushed around? Letting anyone do anything they want to you? Is this what you want?"

I was yelling at that point, yelling so hard my throat hurt. My eyes burned. I only knew I was crying when I felt the hot tears hit my cheeks and smear bright on the black suit before it sucked them into oblivion.

"You know what I want?" I squeezed their shoulders hard. "I want you to say it. Say the safe word. I need to hear it."

You might think I was out of control, but you'd be wrong. I'd never felt more deliberate. I felt like you must feel all the time. Comfortable in my skin. A suit perfectly made only for me.

"Say it," I pushed them harder and they stumbled but remained silent. "Say it!" I slapped their face, not even that hard, but I savoured the velvet sting in my palm. "You love that cat so much, just say his goddamn name."

I stomped across the room, grabbed the corner of the ottoman, and flipped it over. Lazlo crouched frozen and puffed up like a moldy cantaloupe. He yowled when I picked him up, all his disgusting tiny bones poking through his fur into my hands as I held him above my head. "You little bastard, this is all your fault."

V plaintively reached out. For the cat, not me. With a sushi breath howl and prickly contortion, Lazlo twisted out of my grip, raking his claws across my face. I screamed as my eyelid and cheek flamed, and when I felt V's gloves graze my bare back, I lashed out with my fists, swinging wildly as my eye filled with blood.

A punch connected solidly with V's stomach. Another with the side of their head. That void inside me snapped open, and with it a desperate hunger. I tackled them and we fell in a tangle on the floor. Lazlo let out a feral cry behind the tipped over ottoman. I wrapped my hands around V's neck. I squeezed. I stared into the featureless black mask, zipper grinning a huge fuck you back at me. I squeezed harder and realized I had an erection.

Saliva dripped between my grinding teeth as I growled, "Say it."

My aching fingers released their chokehold, and I slammed his head against the hardwood. Then again, harder. Their head bounced. Again. Bounce. Blood from my rent face rained onto that zipper. Again and again, harder and harder, I slammed his head into the floor until instead of bouncing his skull gave with a sick crunch. The tension drained from their body and their limbs flopped open.

"V..." I sat back, still straddling them. "Oh shit, V? Come on..."

Lazlo slithered out from behind the ottoman and mewed pitifully at V's head, nudging and nuzzling. Even sticking out his gross pink tongue and licking the black with a rough scrape of a horsehair brush on denim. But V didn't move. Their chest didn't rise or fall. I'm not sure it ever did, but it definitely wasn't anymore.

Something had gone very wrong.

Lazlo glared.

"What do you want me to do?"

I should've phoned 911. Told them I'm a murderer. But was I?

Lazlo swished his tail. I should have let you take the damn cat.

"Okay, okay…" I pinched the zipper tab between my finger and thumb and that smile chewed itself wide open.

It's no wonder not a single word ever escaped the mask. No wonder you left and took everything. You knew that whatever you left, whatever you gave, it would never be enough. I stared into that hollow maw and it filled my blood-blurred vision until I tumbled into the black. Into dark like you do not know, more empty space than you could ever imagine, the sound of a raspy tongue scraping my ear, and a zipper closing, tooth by tooth.

PRODUCTION UPDATE #2

 **Terry (coordinator)**
September 9, 2021

Some backers have left messages—on the campaign page, Facebook, Twitter, Insta, email, Hotmail, LiveJournal, Parler, Grindr, MySpace, Lumen, AOL, and of course Terrace IV's Sloth Mail—inquiring as to when they will receive their books and assorted rewards. Unfortunately we are still behind due to unforeseen costs and circumstances. Revenue is down due to the pandemic, the price of shrimp is up, and I sustained a concussion when Roy, the angry turtle from Terrace III, slammed a recycling bin lid on my head. He claims I failed to sort my plastics correctly but in fact he is just racist. Anyway, we'll be shipping out soon, as soon as I fix the label printer.

NAKED SAMANATHA

EDDIE GENEROUS

Amber liquid in squat tumblers with ice cubes. Green felt tabletop, cut octagonal. Poker settings in chalky white paint. Five chairs. Four men, trim with jaws cut from stone, hair gelled like turtle shells. Suit jackets cast aside, ties opened, top buttons freed. Two crystal ashtrays cradling four skinny cigars, handcrafted, Dutch. Three of them gone out.

"Better be worth it." Don Hammond is the eldest at thirty-four, spins a diamond-studded pinky ring with an index finger. "Better be worth it."

"My guy, he's good." Terence Winter leans back, eyes on the rustic ceiling fixture as the smoke rises from his mouth to the lightbulb—ghost moth seeking flame.

The building is stone. Has one large bed. Has a kitchenette. Has a simple washroom with a toilet and shower stall. Has windows. Has bars over the windows. Has one door, heavy steel with a keyed deadbolt next to a brushed steel handle. More like a bunker, but not constructed for safety, constructed for the opposite in fact.

"What's the deal? Your guy come here, too?" Clive Murray touches himself through the thin silk of his expensive trousers—Brioni. The shape is clear, sausage under cellophane. "Ready to fuck one of you here in a minute. Your guy always bring'm here?" Clive focuses a fingertip on the damp spot at the tip of his penis.

Terence Winter shrugs, doesn't want to tell them he doesn't know know the man. Spoke in a chatroom. Something about hopeless victims coming right up for help, no work needed. "Calm down, it's not a circle jerk."

"Did that once at Deerfield. Mr. Hanson caught us, but only watched until—"

The door bursts open, cutting off Richard Murdoch's story from high school. A man in black slacks and a black Oxford with a little green Starbucks mermaid over the left breast—told to call him Charlie—pushes a youngish-looking teen through the door. She has on a coat with a fur collar, cheap, polyester. Puffy lips, so sexy they are unbefitting of her innocent visage. Tear streaks cut damp paths down her cheeks. Eyes on the floor. A barista teddy bear wearing a green apron tight in her hands.

"As I promised." Charlie smiles beneath what appears to be a fake beard. Eyes scrunched, authentic pleasure. "Boys, this is Samantha and she was killing time until the bus comes, tomorrow morning's bus, told her she'd be more comfortable here than there." Charlie takes a step backward after this, not waiting for acknowledgement from the Wall Street section, and pulls the door closed. The keyed deadbolt locks from outside.

Terence whistles and stubs out the cigar. Doesn't want to offend their guest.

Clive gets to his feet and unzips the girl's coat. "You don't need this. Warm in here." His hands are rough and busy. He tosses the bear to the floor.

"I'm 'sposed to be at the Rochester station at nine." Samantha lets Clive take her coat, hardly notices the bear. "I'm thirsty. Those candies were bad." She sticks out her tongue after saying this, reveals a bluish skunk stripe. Eyes like saucers.

"A drink, sure." Clive sets her coat on the back of a chair and climbs his hand up her shirt, kneads the small right breast beneath the lightweight bra.

Samantha squirms.

"Be cool." Richard gets to his feet, reaches for Clive's shoulder. "We got all night. Dude ain't coming back 'til morning. Fucking be cool."

Clive unzips his trousers' fly and Samantha's eyes go wide looking at what he's pulling out.

"Cool the fuck out!" Don has Clive by the neck, reefs him back to the bed. "You nasty bastard, you'll scare her." Don turns his face to Samantha. "You okay, honey?"

Samantha shakes her head. Of course she's not.

"Get her one of those." Don snaps his fingers, pointing at the Bacardi coolers, ignoring the hard sneer coming from Clive on the bed.

Terence holds out the orange bottle. It's cool, drinkable if you have a taste for candy. "Here, girl. We won't let Clive do anything—"

"Like fuck! I paid! Same as all you!" Clive is up to his feet, fly open, but penis stowed.

Don turns, furrows his brow, his forehead a plowed skin field. "What's wrong with you? You psycho. We can't break her. We gotta put her back." Don faces Samantha, leaning a bit for a shared eye-level. "You're safe. We're just gonna drink some drinks and all have a good time, promise. Do you believe me?"

Samantha's bottom lip and chin quiver. Her hands wrap around the Bacardi Breezer bottle. She shakes her head.

"Girl. Samantha. You can trust me. We'll all have a good time. Even you. I know you're scared, but trust me, okay?" Don holds out his right hand, palm up.

Samantha pauses, makes a crying face, but shakes it off, takes Don's hand.

"Good. Sit. You like games?" Don takes his spot while guiding Samantha into the spot made vacant when Clive lost his head. "You like cards?"

Samantha shrugs.

"Take a sip." Don motions to the bottle.

Samantha looks at the men, checking every face twice in a rotating half-circle. She isn't going to drink. She's too scared. She's...she sips. The tension falls.

Terence picks up the cards. "Let's keep it easy, Texas Hold'm. How much money you got?" He's grinning at Samantha.

She makes the cry face again.

"No worries! Simpler yet. So cozy in here, we can bet clothes and won't get cold." Terence is shuffling the deck, the crotch of his pants swelling in anticipation.

"No way, no way. Can't strip." Samantha takes a fourth sip. Her cheeks are rosy.

"Guess you better win, eh?" Richard winks at her.

Clive's sneer has his upper lip curled, eyetooth unhidden. "Yeah, you better."

"Cool it." Terence starts dishing, dealing Samantha's hand from the bottom. Flips junk but for an ace on the flop.

"Finish that and I'll grab you another." Don is already halfway to standing.

Samantha doesn't argue and drains the stuff. Tastes like Creamsicle. She hasn't picked up her cards, too out of it to observe that the men have. "I like it." Her belly is warm as her cheeks, warmer even. Tingly all over.

Don sets down a new bottle and then freshens all the tumblers with whiskey, but not ice. The ice is in the kitchen on the other side of the table, ignored. Like the cigars. The cigars have become room dressing. "Look at your cards." He points to Samantha's hand. The neck of her second Bacardi is empty.

"Minimum, one piece of clothing." Terence holds the card stack and drops a second ten, this one hearts. "Bets?"

Richard wraps knuckles on the table.

Clive stands. "Raise one." Opens the button on his pants.

Don waves. "Drop'm when you lose."

Clive tuts.

Don tosses his cards. "Fold."

The focus is on Samantha. "I don't know what to do."

"I'll help." Don leans over, looks at Samantha's cards, smirks at Terence. "You're gonna want to call him."

She shrugs and drinks, holding her cards willy-nilly against the glass. Only Clive across the table can't see.

Terence tosses his cards.

Richard tosses his cards.

Terence flips the river card, another ace, spades.

Clive doesn't even consider the offering, his cards face down flat, his palms on the table. "Raise."

Samantha turns to Don, serious concern knitting her girlish features—helplessness incarnate.

"Take him down." Don nods at Clive. "Show'm."

Clive, still sneering, flips two tens. "Four of a fucking kind. Take it off, you little tease."

The others erupt into laughter. All knew what was what. Don takes the two aces from Samantha's hand. "Oops." He takes off his shirt, leaves the tie.

Terence takes off a sock.

Richard takes off his tie.

Clive strips to his boxers, socks, and button-up.

The clothes sit in a mound in front of Samantha and she's smiling, lips orange, cheeks aflame. "I won? I won! Woo!"

Richard, less adept at stacking a hand, still manages to keep the good times going. Samantha reaps the benefits.

Clive plays with his slightly engorged penis below the table. He keeps on his socks and tie, sick of the foreplay, but being cool. When it's his turn to deal, no hand is stacked.

"You're a thirsty girl." Don gets up and grabs another bottle.

"It's good. I'm all hot." Samantha rubs between her thighs in the Y shaped shadow at the crotch of her jeans, like the booze knew where to go, where the men needed it to go so they didn't have to get rough. Not too rough anyway. "I'm spinny."

Terence nods at the bottle. "Take that one slower."

Samantha smiles at him. "You're hairy. Is it soft?"

Terence sticks out his chest, runs fingers through the hair, smiles. "Pretty soft. Feel it."

Samantha reaches over and plays two fingers down almost to his bellybutton. She giggles. "It is soft."

"Let's go." Clive's dealt and waiting.

Samantha bets to the end. The pile of winnings is halved.

Don deals.

Samantha bets to the end. There's no pile left. "Oh. I don't know."

"Don't know what?" Don's shuffling the cards.

"I can't lose my clothes. I need them, okay? Maybe we played enough. I mean. Okay?" Samantha pulls at her shirtfront for emphasis. Lips puckered small and eyebrows raised.

Don shakes his head. "Sorry, girl. Not fair." He tosses cards before her.

Samantha doesn't understand folding. She's tipping to and fro, her eyes glazed, looking swimmy. She huffs, angry when she has to lose her coat and socks.

The dealer spot skips her. The men have their clothes back, but haven't put them on.

She loses.

Don puts a hand on her knee.

She loses.

Terence smells the seat of the pants he's won.

She loses.

"Stand up." Clive is tugging himself below the table, his voice a hiss, heartbeat in his words, hummingbirding. "Stand up and show." The sounds from under the table are wet and smacky.

Samantha's crying, shaking her head. No. Has on only white cotton panties. Has her arms folded over her nubbin breasts.

Don waves to placate Clive, deals Samantha trash. His hand goes back to her thigh, higher up. The heat coming off that secret space has him hard as a rock. "Don't worry, you can bet with kisses and clothes." He squeezes a little, has to bite his lower lip to reel it in some.

The cards come out and Samantha loses. She's crying and shaking her head as Terence helps her to her feet. Don has his nose between her thighs, rolling the panties down, savoring.

"Three kisses to the winner, and I pick where. I wanted all-in, but we can play slow. We can." Terence pulls down his boxer shorts and a stiff red penis springs free.

"No. No, but...no." Samantha is shaking all over.

"Yes." Clive is on his feet, really pulling himself, about to release on the cards and the green felt of the table.

"No!" Samantha has hands on her, feeling the merchandise. She starts convulsing, more like a cat with a hairball than a scared little girl vomiting up Bacardi.

Don backs a step.

Terence leans away.

Richard has wide, patient eyes. Into watching more than anything else.

"Bring her here. I wanna cum on her face." Clive's body is rigid and cords are sticking out in his neck, in his arms, and in his legs. "Hurry. Hurry." He's panting, ratcheting his arm like a piston.

Samantha falls back into her chair as a pale pink balloon spreads her lips wide open and slides to the table. The balloon is flesh. The balloon, it moves. The veins and arteries, the steady in and out of the impossible breaths.

"What the fuck?" Terence pops in reverse, sending his chair over.

Samantha isn't finished, but she no longer looks helpless or sad. Something's changed. She reaches a hand down her throat and pulls out the other balloon, other lung. "With the underwear, that's three. All-in?" The lungs breathe steady on the tossed card pile. "How much I owe? How much? All-in?"

Clive shakes, too far along, and starts cumming on the table. "What the hell?" His words are high, whining, tailing into a dog whistle. "What the hell?"

"All-in?" Samantha spreads her legs, revealing what the men had plans of tenderizing, that veal steak. She digs to her elbow and pulls.

Pink and red. The shiny flesh spills. Uterus. Bladder. Urethra. Cervix. Some of it holds steady to her, dangles. A pink sock. The floor is glossy with guts.

Don breaks for the door and starts pulling. The deadbolt needs a key. "Fuck this. Fuck this." The windows are barred and his eyes bounce to the options that aren't options at all.

Clive is on the bed. Curled.

"All-in!" Samantha digs fingernails into her breasts and tears the flesh in huge strips that coil off her, leather cinnamon buns, but massive. "All-in!" She reaches around muscles and her ribcage and pulls free her still-beating heart, tosses it to Richard, who catches it and hot potatoes it at Terence. "All-in!"

The men are screaming. They've retreated to corners, helpless little boys playing a game they weren't prepared to play.

The moon out the window shows midnight. Samantha is all bones and eyes and brains and hair. The men are on the bed, mostly naked, huddled together. They've said little since they'd stopped screaming. Since she'd stopped digging around muscles and started stripping them away instead.

"I'll fucking sue you." Clive has his knees up, his shrivelled scrotum poking out between his thighs above the hairy crack of his ass. He'd covered his face when Samantha slammed a kidney on the tabletop, almost an hour earlier, and then pointed at him. Hasn't quit shivering, knowing something. Knowing there's more coming.

Richard nudges Clive. "Shut the fuck up. Shut the fuck up, you goddamned tool." Hardly a whisper, trying to avoid the attention of the thing sitting on a chair at the poker table.

"This can't be real." Don rocks gently.

Terence lights a fresh cigar off the one he's just finished. Chain relief. But not really relieving at all. "What are—?"

The deadbolt tumbles and the door opens. The men's faces lighten when they see Charlie, but darken when he locks the door after entering.

"You're dead." Clive is peeking out from the crook of his elbow.

Charlie shrugs. "No. Not me."

Samantha's skeleton, her eyes—above their trailing nerve tendrils—follow the man's movements.

The spleen is first. Charlie digs through the mound of wet tissue and picks it up. He presses it to his lips, his fake beard going pink around the mouth—zombie Santa lookalike. He sets the organ inside Samantha's bone cage. "I love you one." It floats in the exactly right spot. He picks up the stomach, kisses it. "I love you two."

"What in the fuck?" Don's teeth chatter around the words.

Charlie ignores him and keeps going. Picks up a kidney, sniffs it, makes a face, and tosses it aside. "Rotten." Pulls a knife like an oversized scalpel within a leather sheath from a deep hip pocket.

Samantha points to Clive.

The blade salutes. "You want to live, you'll hold him down."

The men exchange glances.

Clive jumps. "No!"

They grab him.

Charlie cuts. Crude. There's too much blood.

The other men still hope. Each still hopes.

Don loses a lung. Wheezing. "Gone to sew me up. Right?"

Terence loses his small intestine. The large intestine coils in his lap, his hands greedy with need to shove it back in. Too slick.

Richard is scared. Samantha needs a new heart. "No. I'll die." His hands wave and swat.

"Behave." Charlie pins him and plunges the blade.

Whines. A death rattle. Wheezing. The bed, puddled red.

Charlie continues the good work. Putting Samantha back together, doing the ritual that completes not only her, but him too.

An abdominal oblique. "I love you twenty-one."

The rectum. "I love you three hundred."

Her lips. "I love you eight hundred and nine."

Samantha runs that tongue over her lips. "I love you, too." Those lips shift into something playful, her childlike visage momentarily flashed, but is then stolen away. "I hope you survive for days. I really do."

"What?" Clive is on his knees, bloody hands out, begging. "You can't. Please, I'll do anything."

"That's the problem with your kind." Samantha plucks items of her wardrobe from the floor. Then her barista bear. Then Charlie takes her hand and they step to the door.

She's out first, he's following, glances over his shoulder. "You think you're suffering now?" He locks the door. The sound of the shouting men trails them to the car, but no further.

Samantha takes Charlie's hand and kisses it. "Thank you."

"Thank you." Charlie kisses her back, starts the engine, and rolls.

PRODUCTION UPDATE #3

 **Terry (coordinator)**
December 31, 2021

First off, I apologize for the lack of communication. Months ago, I'd promised we'd be shipping out right away. However I've been dealing with some health issues in the form of the aforementioned concussion from Roy, the wrathful turtle, and a tenacious strain of HPV from Gary. I told you penguins will fuck anything, and Gary in particular has fucked everything. I'm struggling with depression. I can barely eat eight hundred pounds of shrimp in a sitting. But, I'm working twenty-seven hours a day to get back on track. Except the shipping label printer is fucked. Please consider backing our Crowdfunder for a new printer.

Happy New Year!

FAT APOCALYPSE

ROBIN VAN ECK

The mailman is stealing our flyers. We're sure of it. We stand on our patio and wait for him to pull up on the street, flop out of the red and white van with a *thwump*, and waddle up to the boxes. He pours in letters and cards and parcels, but no flyers.

The world wasn't always this way. No need to hoard and scrimp for paper and organic scraps. But then it happened. Oil prices plummeted, the cost of produce sky-rocketed, related or not, people struggled to survive. Pinching pennies, making meals stretch, eating cheap even if it means going for the least nutritious options. The people became groggy and unsatisfied. Loping through the supermarket aisles, passing the lettuce and broccoli florets with not so much as a sniff. Dazed and misguided. Canned goods and Cocoa Puffs leapt off the shelves, burrowed into their shopping carts.

Waistlines stretched. Buttons strained and popped.

We try not to think about what came next.

Across the street, a fat burden of a man lives with his morbidly obese dog. He's a waster. Tosses cans and jars into the street. Doesn't finish his TV dinners. Frozen globs of imitation food adhere to the microwave-safe containers as he drops them into plastic garbage bags and dusts off his hands. So much plastic. Disregarded. Non-biodegradable.

His window is wide open. It's hard not to look. The dog stumbles around the living room, parking his rump wherever his little legs give out. The man reclines on the couch, his mass absorbing the cushions. Empty 2L bottles of cream soda lay at his feet.

We first encountered the man in the public washroom of the Hurry Inn and Diner on the QEII highway, just outside the city. Rows of semis hauling loaded trailers filled the parking lot, drivers pulled over to dust away the road wearies and slurp down noodles and hot sauce. We'd stopped to relieve our bulging bladders and retrieve a cold beverage from the machine. The man pulled in, driving his rust bucket VW van, fell from the vehicle and sauntered to the toilets, hiking his pants up. Not nearly as big then as he is now, but tired from the miles between there and here, he pushed into the bathroom ahead of us. A dirty joint, with piss stains dripping from clogged porcelain, urinal cakes long disintegrated. He ignored the rows of pissers and wedged himself into a stall where his bowels splashed into the bowl. A satisfied sigh slid from under the door.

"Needs a nice green salad."

"Would scare the bejeezus out of his organs."

No one can afford that luxury now. If we don't grow it, we don't eat it. At risk of becoming chemically imbalanced zombies, held together by high fructose corn syrup. Our own personal salt licks.

Among the trees in our backyard we hide, nurture and cultivate vegetables of all varieties. Raised garden boxes made from wooden pallets grow carrots, celery, tomatoes, potatoes, radishes, eggplant, squash and cucumber. The garage that used to stand at the far back corner of the yard, full of unused tools, snowmobiles, a '70 Challenger on blocks, has been demolished, the boards used to create a barrier between them and us. Our garden oasis. Cultivate and hoard. Untouchable.

We slip along the rows, watering, plucking weeds. They flourish. We flourish. While mounds of malnutrition stomp through the streets, their glucose levels bottoming out, moaning and grumbling to one another. They'd eat their hats if they could stomach the roughage.

Rarely a need to go out. Except now. Our paper pile wanes and we're down to the last cup of compost. We refuse to become cardboard cut outs of Uncle Ben and Tony the Tiger.

We nod to each other. It's time.

In the basement, we pull out our suits, dyed black to blend with the night. We seal each other's arms and ankles with copious rolls of duct tape and secure masks made of soda bottles, electrical tape and furnace filters. Then out into the night, down the alley, past other houses where the occupants snort and burp and fart.

Our feet squelch and stick to the asphalt as we weave through an obstacle course of discarded wrappers and sewage burbling in the gutters. Even through our masks, we can smell the shit and depression wedged into the ruts in the road, its tangled arms reaching, beckoning, clawing.

In choreographed steps, we dart into the street, alert for signs of movement. Dusk is settling, the sidewalks empty during Jeopardy hour, Big Brother to follow. Two hours to scavenge, collect, and get back home, before we are spotted.

Garbage receptacles overflow, flooding the streets with plastic and genetically modified leftovers: bread crusts, donuts with bites marks, factory formed vegetables that turn to powder when they dry. Unclipping our cloth bags from our belts, we sift through the refuse. One bag for paper: cardboard, tissues, napkins, newspapers. Real organic matter, hard to come by. Not even a coffee ground to be found. One street, then another, our hopes disintegrate.

A *scrape, shuffle, shuffle* stops us in our tracks. We glance at each other—shhh—and sink into the shadowed awning of the Book Nook, the windows shaken from their frames, the store ransacked. Not so much as a bookmark remains, we checked. We peer around the corner, searching for the source of the noise—any scuffle, sneeze, or snort. The signal of the oncoming herd.

They said no one could have predicted it. But we did. The way the obese and dissatisfied lumbered along the streets, standing on street corners, peering at one another through pinhole eyes. The air changed.

That day, we drifted through the farmer's market stocking up on greens and AAA beef, hormone free chicken and eggs.

"It's organic," the woman at the vegetable stand said, a smile scraping her face. She held a ripe red tomato in the cup of her hands. "Isn't it the most precious thing you ever saw?"

And then the ornamental garden gnomes began to shudder. Storefronts shattered, foundations cracked, a fire hydrant ruptured. A Coca Cola truck raided, fizzy soda pop spraying their skin as they slurped and sucked. Mothers clutched their babies, covered their eyes, hid under produce stands. The doors were barricaded and we waited until dawn, when they finally tired, their stomachs gurgling, their IBS flaring.

Now, the stains have faded, bubble gum pressed flat into the pavement. But every night, at exactly the same time, they unfold themselves from the cushions, unplug from their daze, and rumble through the streets and only once the siren sounds, do they return.

No clue what it all means. Don't know where they go. And don't want to find out. We glance up and down the dark roadway. The clock tower stuck on 9:00. The hour, the exact minute, of the fat apocalypse.

"Let's go."

We tiptoe from our hiding places, clinging to the shadows. Our bags aren't even close to full.

Around the corner and past a Co-Op with the lights still blazing, we pause, glance at one another.

The glass doors slide open, hitting us with a gust of lukewarm air. Bins that once held mounds of colourful fresh fruit now filled with bags of Factory made chalky substitutes, painted in artificial colours that look grey under the fluorescent lights. Fake grapes hard as marbles, cauliflower cut from a mould, pumped full of steroids and a gelatinous substance to hold their shape.

The government said it was necessary. Cut costs. Save the people. Now there's only freezer-burned meat, not worthy of any grade. Dairy fridges empty but standing on an end cap, boxes of powdered milk and yogurt, a dehydrated cheese substance. Just add water.

We grab a box of corn flakes from the cereal aisle. Don't even touch the canned vegetables. Check for paper products, but the aisle is mostly empty. The others like us—and there aren't many—have emptied the shelves. Not even a stray lightbulb or battery. A few Swiffers, cans of lemon Pledge. We find a roll of misplaced toilet paper and tuck it into our bag. At the front of the store, a lone woman stands at the checkout, colouring her nails black with a permanent marker. She's so skinny her jaw juts from under her skin, eyes sunk deep into sockets, red smock barely clinging to her shoulders. She gives us a lazy glance, coughs up a wad of phlegm and turns back to her nails.

"Newspapers?" we ask.

She coughs again and points to a stand by the deserted customer service counter. Jackpot. We fill our bags with all the newspaper we can carry and hightail it out of the store.

"You gonna pay for those?" The woman doesn't follow.

Outside, we retrace our steps, eyes alert, skin bristling at the imagined click, click of channels changing, TV's shutting down. We turn onto our street and stop in our tracks.

The man from across the street looms in front of us, the drooling dog at his side. The man's mouth opens and closes. No words come out. His teeth caked with yellow matter, his tongue, too big for his mouth, lolls to one side. Crumbs rest in the folds of his chin. The eyes open and close, trying to focus. Rolls spill from the top of his pants. A determined hunger in his eyes to match the grumbling in his gut. The man reaches out a meaty hand, a groan erupts from his throat, and he lunges forward. But we are two and he is only one. We part and deke from his grasp. The man rears back, his feet stamp the ground, nostrils flare. The dog wobbles forward, teeth bared.

And as if on cue, the streets are suddenly overcome with jellied flesh. We scramble for cover. A hand grabs the back of our suits and we are lifted, then dragged like a sack of potatoes. We kick and scratch to no avail. Tree trunk thighs on either side of us, jiggling bellies, sprays of spittle mixed with chunks of food and Red Dye 40.

The street blurs. We can't breathe. The suits are digging into our necks, reducing our O2 supply.

We wake in air thick as curdled milk and smells even worse. No light. A small compartment. No sound. We lift off our masks—cringe at the sulphur stench—grope in the dark, legs folded tight, unable to stretch. Our hands touch steel. Something digs into our backs. Shifting, we feel the treads of an old tire. A trunk?

We listen for a murmur. A scrape. Any sign we are not alone, but the silence deepens.

"Don't make a sound."

"We're screwed."

We brace our legs against the trunk and push. Milky yellow light seeps through the crack, but something is holding it closed. It's no use. We are freezer-burned chicken drumsticks in plastic wrap with nothing to do but wait to be thawed.

"They will eat us."

"We're not processed enough."

The car bobs up and down, a grunt and a groan, and the lid lifts a sliver.

We push open the lid and see the rounded rump of a man disappear into the dark. We sit up, gulping air. "That was close." We nod at each other and climb out.

A large iron gate looms in front of us—Welcome to the Greatest Outdoor Show on Earth—against a cloudless, moonless sky.

We should leave, but something pulls us through the gate. A familiar smell. The stank suggestion of boiled tenderloin, and—we glance at each other—apple pie. Cracked neon signs flicker, sparks erupt and sizzle on the wet concrete.

Past an abandoned ticket booth, the price of admission long since faded, along a deserted walk that might have been the midway in another lifetime. Tents have been erected in even rows on either side, front flaps closed tight. A Ferris wheel car dangles from unoiled hinges, the screech and scrape shattering the silence. We pass a life-sized wooden sign with a cowboy painted on the front, a red gloved hand waving.

"What have they done to the place?"

"Creepy as shit."

Deeper we go, careful to stay to the middle in case someone busts from one of the tents. Music seeps into the night, thick as gravy, enchanting. Seductive. Around a corner, a row of empty cages, seven in total, large enough to trap a tiger. The doors hang open.

The music grows louder. Down the midway, the path narrows and light spills from a building, unearthly shadows move in a monstrous dance.

"What on earth?" Something catches our eye in the last cage.

The floor is layered with straw. A ladies shoe, red, missing the heel, sits in the corner, its match, long since departed.

"Don't like this at all."

We hear snuffling around our feet. The dog appears from between two cages, sniffing the ground. It stops, tilts its head up at us and pees.

From the shadows, murmurs. Whispers. Grunts.

The music grows louder.

"They're going to cut off our heads and mount them on sticks."

"If we're lucky."

A familiar smell pulls us closer, something long forgotten: baked goods. Our mouths water as we approach the door. We squint in the light, blistering hot. Our mouths drop open. Naked mounds of male flesh undulate in the spicy air, glistening with oil or sweat, it's hard to tell. Man boobs jostle, their itty bitty parts covered with coconut husks, half a cantaloupe, presumably scraped out, attached to their heads by a string wound under their chins. Their eyes are closed, menacing grins stretch across their faces.

A tray of dinner rolls is thrust into our laps.
"Eat."

The music turns to a banjo strum, high energy. Any moment Yankee Doodle may appear, waving around a feather, bouncing on his donkey. It's impossible to avert our eyes, though we want desperately to do just that.

We grab squishy buns and rip them in half, savouring the exquisite texture, ripe with gluten, soft dough melting over our tongues. Real. Unprocessed. Where'd all this come from?

"A little butter would be nice."

Rectangles of brick cover the opposite wall, floor to ceiling. A large black door opens to reveal raging flames. Sheets of pastries are pulled from the oven and placed on a long wooden table. More buns, strudels, pies in all flavours imaginable. Large women scrape bowls of lard into tubs of flour. A hum fills the air as giant mixers grind and gyrate, sending clouds of flour into the air.

The man from across the street waddles up to us, face so close we can see up his nose. His cantaloupe slides to the side of his head. "You like?" His chins undulate with the words. "Dance." A belly laugh starts low in his gut and curls up and up until it sounds like he's choking on his tongue.

The music changes again, into a chipmunk version of the Conga, giant hands grip our waists and thrust us forward, the rhythm of the music getting stronger, we kick our feet. Once around and then we are thrust into the middle of the circle, a sumo stomping ring around us. Heat blazes from the oven, sweat streams down our faces. We rip off the suits and cling to each other. An opening appears in the circle and a woman steps forward, watermelon shells cover her breasts and a thong made of Cling Wrap and sanitary napkins cover her other parts.

"Take off your clothes," she says.

Our hearts are ready to tear from our chests, but we strip nude, clothes tossed with our protective suits. The woman lathers our bodies with oil, no part left uncovered and then two halves of a cantaloupe land at our feet. She looks down and then back at us and then down again.

"You're kidding, right?"

"We're going to be baked."

A smile tugs at her lips, her eyes brighten a moment and then she stalks out of the circle, the hole closing behind her.

The man from across the street steps forward and straps the cantaloupes to our heads.

"Now. We feast."

The corral of bodies loosens and we are left standing, stark naked.

"Do we get a...you know...coconut, too?"

He yanks us to the long table of food and forces us to our knees. There're chickens, at least a dozen, cooked golden brown, a turkey with all the fixings, green beans, peas, carrots, potatoes, roasted in garlic and dripping with butter. Bowls of dinner rolls, plates of brownies, butter tarts, crème brulee.

"Eat. Eat. Eat."

The mashed potatoes, exquisite. The turkey melts on our tongues. More and more. We can't stop.

"Eat. Eat. Eat." The chant grows louder. "Eat. Eat. Eat."

Our skin begins to stretch. Expand. We want to stop. We can't.

And then, a shrill siren slices the air. We clamp our hands over our ears. The music stops. The fires snap out. The tent dissolves into nothing more than canvas flaps. The plates, once overflowing, are now full of gelatin-like substances, grey crumbs of food we don't recognize.

The grumbling bodies dress and begin to file out the door, leaving trails of oil behind them. The man from across the street pauses and turns, beckons with a meaty hand, his dog sniffing at our privates.

PRODUCTION UPDATE #4

 **Terry (coordinator)**
February 30th, 2022

I regret to inform our backers that we've been hacked. For the last few weeks I've been attempting to recover data while caring for my ailing Parrot. They say a bird can't love a fish, and sure enough Linda drowned yesterday. I am gutted, friends. Devastated. As if that weren't enough, due to ongoing label printer issues I've been writing out addresses by hand, no easy task when all you've got is fins, and as a result I've developed a repetitive strain injury. But I won't let my grief or my disability get in the way of my promise to get these books out. Keep an eye on your mailboxes!

CHEESEBURGER PHILOSOPHY

ROBERT BOSE

Ever wonder why people love cheap, fast food hamburgers? Woofing them down and licking the processed cheese from crinkled wax paper too thin to contain the oozing toxic waste? I'll tell you why. They're fucking delicious, a god damn religious experience, each semi-identical brand a cult ready to snuff the guy who prefers the competition's faux-meat patty or toasted brioche bun. Maybe not war in the streets, though as incumbents slide into memory and next wave innovators spring up, you know it's coming. God help their lard asses and bursting arteries.

I'm not being facetious. God cares more than you'd think. She's mellowed since the old times, packed away her thunderbolts and plagues and floods. Decided to give redemption another go. Absolution 2.0. More a do-over of numero uno if you ask me, but of course she didn't. Never does. That's why I'm standing in this alley, stubbing a Marlboro against a peeling doorframe and swirling a foot through ankle deep trash, aforementioned burger wrappers comprising the lion's share.

"Jesus Christ," I mumble, eyes watering from the stench.

"Yeah?"

The lid slams shut as a lean, shirtless man staggers out of the doorway, long, black curls framing his middle-eastern face and scruffy beard. The King. He takes a bite from a dripping cheeseburger — the wax paper wrapper kin to those swirling around my shoes — and wipes a grimy hand across his little potbelly. I light another cigarette and take a long drag.

"Smoke went up from his nostrils, and devouring fire from his mouth; glowing coals flamed forth from him."

Here he goes again. Nattering. Always with the bloody nattering. I'd kill for three days of peace and quiet.

"You should get cleaned up," I say.

"Wash me, and I shall be whiter than snow." He grins, crooked teeth glowing in the setting sun.

"King James Version again? At least pick a decent Greek translation."

He shrugs, jams the rest of the burger down his throat, and tosses the crumpled wrapper to the ground.

"And remember your manners." I point to the wrapper. "I know this is a shit-hole, but quit being an asshole."

I'm preaching again dammit, but he doesn't care, wandering the desert in search of meaning that eludes the entire extended family, both upstairs and down.

"Making the best use of the time, because the days are evil."

I look him over. A couple of fresh bruises, already fading. Split lip. Bloody knuckles. The local talent must be thinner than usual. "Round two already?"

He nods and goes back inside the roadhouse, humming a 70's B-side Black Sabbath tune. Wicked World?

I follow and ease onto a stool at the end of the bar. There's a small crowd around a dance floor flanked by worn, wooden chairs and the King leans against the jukebox, looking bored, listening to a tall, bald reject from ZZ Top explain the rules to a wiry hillbilly having trouble unbuttoning his gator skin vest. Another hillbilly, obviously his moron brother, is attempting to help. I turn back to the bar when someone starts talking at me.

"Doesn't look like much, but I hear your boy can throw a mean right."

The bartender I'd met earlier, while having my first half dozen drinks of the evening, is gone. In his place is an older guy. Slicked back hair. Flat black suit and narrow tie straight out of a Tarantino movie.

"He's too stupid to know when to quit, if that's what you're asking."

"Aren't they all, aren't they all. The name's Simon, Simon Sloane. I own this here establishment." He thrusts out his hand.

I shake it. "Gabe."

"Of course, of course. Well Gabe, we'll get your boy warmed up on some of the local wannabes and hit the main event tomorrow night. A hundred for each win tonight, fifty for a loss, which, based on your rep, isn't going to happen. Five hundred tomorrow if he can put down Samson, the local champ."

I shrug, rolling my shoulders and lean forward across the bar top. There's a stack of coasters next to a bowl of peanuts so I palm a moist cardboard circle and spin it between my fingers, admiring the elaborate artwork from some local craft distillery. "Sure." The money isn't important.

"I've never seen someone as... imposing as you." He cranes his head, gives me a once over. "You fight?"

"Sometimes."

"You got the look. Where you from? I mean originally, France?"

He's trying to place my sorta yet non-Cajun accent, which does have a trace of French rolling around in it, along with a few hundred others. I give him a half-nod; it'll make him happy to think he's perceptive.

"More importantly, where the hell do you find clothes that fit?"

I grunt a laugh.

He grins, pleased. "Well, looks like the fight's going to start, can I get you something?"

"Bourbon. Corsair Triple Smoke if you have any."

"Ha, where do you think you are, the Big Easy? We have Old Grand-Dad and Yellow Label and uh," he pulls down a bottle from the back of the top shelf, "a half of Makers."

"That'll do."

The bearded guy climbs onto a chair and clears his throat, hushing the room. "Ladies and Gentleman." He looks around. "Gentlemen. Our good friend Caleb, fresh in from Dulac, has expressed his intentions to take on the out-of-towner. After mopping the floor with poor Joseph earlier, everyone welcome the King, straight from a tour of Texas and before that, the Holy Land. Place your bets."

There's a bit of hollering, a couple of claps, a couple of muttered rag-head comments, but everyone starts handing the announcer fistfuls of green.

Caleb bounces up and down, jabbing, while the King watches with a bent smile.

There's a rustle and I swivel back to the bar when Simon drops a glass onto a coaster and pours a couple of fingers. "Want me to leave the bottle?"

"Sure, why the hell not."

We watch Caleb throw a few punches, hitting nothing but air, while his brother yells encouragement.

"Levi and Caleb, quite the pair, aren't they? Dumb as stumps, but they do bring a jug of enthusiasm." Simon snags a rag and begins wiping down the gleaming bar top.

The King ducks a wild roundhouse and drills Caleb in the stomach. One. Two. After a third for good measure, the hillbilly folds, vomit leaking from the corner of his mouth onto his muck stained boots. His brother pulls him up and pats his back. Whispers in his ear. There's a nod, a narrowing of wounded animal eyes.

"Oh, that's gotta hurt. You set up at the motel?" asks Simon.

"Yeah."

"Good, good."

Caleb blows his nose on a rag and spits. Puts his head down and rushes, long sinewy arms flailing like tentacles. The King sees it coming and dances out of the way, taking the opportunity to smash an elbow into the side of the man's face. The crunch reverberates through the bar and all eyes follow Caleb as he stumbles, forward motion propelling him into the wall. A chair arm catches his head on his way down and two kinds of wood hit the floor with a clatter.

Levi hurries over and shakes, but his brother is out, finished. The swamp slang flows as Levi gets up and into the King's face. Without a word, a casual right cross leaves the second brother on the floor. There's a couple of boos, frowns and smiles, and a flurry of bills change hands.

"Ha, ha! Would you look at that? Two for the price of one." Simon reaches out to slap my shoulder, but thinks better of it and shifts to adjust an autographed picture of Charlton Heston on the wall. "Well, let me know if you need anything, anything at all, and I'll make it happen."

I knock back the bourbon and snag the bottle. "Thanks, appreciated."

He nods, gives a sage little smile, and wanders into the back. The King joins me at the bar, rubbing his knuckles and massaging his elbow.

"What did the guy hiss at you before you smoked him?"

"I will raise my fist against you, to roll you down from the heights. When I am finished, you will be nothing but a heap of rubble. You will be desolate forever. Even your stones will never again be used for building. You will be completely wiped out."

"So, the usual."

He nods and pulls on a stained White Savior t-shirt, digs another cheeseburger from a brown paper bag, and begins chewing loudly, mouth half open. An older blonde, hard, pretty, and layered in unnecessary makeup saddles up behind the bar. Smiles at us. Him.

"Bonjour. I'm Mary-Jane. MJ to most. What'cha need?"

The King holds up what remains of his burger.

"Heart-attack special from Missy's Frostop. She'll be closin' soon, but I'll see what I can do."

She looks up at me. "And you?"

I fill my glass from the bottle. "I'm good."

With hips swaying, she sashays to the end of the bar and hollers at a waitress while the King grins. "She is like the ships of the merchant; she brings her food from afar."

I tuck drifting pale hair behind an ear. Twist on my stool. "Really? You're not going there, are you? She's—"

"Behold, you are beautiful, my love; behold, you are beautiful; your eyes are doves."

"Look, I told your father I'd watch over you, keep you out of trouble this go around, but you're pulling the exact same shit as last time. Why can't you take this seriously?"

The look I get breaks my heart. If his work was difficult two thousand years ago, it's a million times harder now. There's little he can say, little he can do to save a world that doesn't want to be saved. Once in a while, when he's sated on burgers and two sheets to the wind, he holds up his scarred hands and stares through them. "Gabriel," he whispers, "Am I forsaken?"

I can't answer that. All I know is we've both been left with impossible obligations.

The King reaches out, plucks an errant silver-white feather from my shirtsleeve. Cups it in his hand and blows it towards Mary-Jane busy serving the local drunks lined up at the far end of the bar, as far from us as possible.

"Let her be as the loving hind and pleasant roe; let her breasts satisfy thee at all times; and be thou ravished always with her love."

The bottle of bourbon makes its way into his hand and he raises it. Toasts. Guzzles the remaining ounces.

🔥

The screaming reaches my ears long before I get to the motel room door. Screaming. Screeching. Banging. Shit loads of banging.

"Oh God, oh GOD, OOOOOHHHH GOD."

She has absolutely no idea. I lean against the wall and light up a smoke, listen to the slap of meat on meat, listen to the raspy sharp breath as they finish.

"That was amazing, Chéri," she purrs.

"Glad you could take time out of your busy schedule to provide such wonderful hospitality." He's matching her, using his English accent now. The charming one he reserves for special occasions. The sharp slap of hand on ass echoes into the parking lot.

A giggle. Then a cough and I hear her spit. "Why is your bed full of feathers?"

"This is Gabe's bed, ask him. He might even tell you if you bring him a drink."

"He bust open a pillow or something? You should call housekeeping."

"Later, love. Later. First, have you ever been to India?"

"No. I've always wanted to, but—" There's desire in her voice. Regret.

"Then let me show you a little thing I picked up in Khajuraho a long time ago."

She draws a sharp breath. Moans. "Oh… god…"

I toss my butt to the concrete. Grind it out. My bed, my goddamn bed. He does it on purpose to fire me up, knows I prefer the finer things and delights when I have to follow him through the muck, down at the level where he's decided his best chances to make a difference are.

To tell the truth I didn't mind at first. There's a certain thrill in scraping the bottom of the barrel, but I didn't reckon on the futility of it all and having to watch him self-destruct as he realized it too.

Nobody gives a shit anymore. If they ever did.

I walk across the street to the roadhouse in search of another drink. It's past midnight, but they never shut down. Eternal southern hospitality, the kind of heaven I'm going to miss when it all goes to hell.

Samson turns out to be a thick-necked goliath. He struts in, long curls bouncing, arms flush with tattoos, sporting a wife beater and a retinue of biker chicks. He wastes no time finding the King where he's sitting, and, of course, eating.

"I'm going to crush you, you greasy little motherfucker."

The King smiles, but I laugh loud enough for both of them to hear. Samson strides over and flexes his arms.

"You. I want you, not that little shit. He may be able handle some idiot moonshiners, but Saturday night is for the gods. I heard you crushed Franklin in Lake Charles. It's meant to be, you and I."

"No."

"Come on. I'm sure Simon'll make it worth your while. Double, at least. And I can see it in your eyes. The hunger. You're hungry, aren't you?"

I stand up. He's big, but I have an inch on him. I take off my sunglasses for the first time this weekend and look him in the eyes. He doesn't like the revelation.

"I tell you what," I say. "You take the King, shut him up for the rest of the weekend, and we'll dance."

"I..." He backs away and lifts a hand as his entourage mills nervously, expectant. "I'll hold you to that."

"I'll be here, don't worry yourself." I fill my glass and hold it up. Nod at him. "Cheers, motherfucker."

He spins and retreats across the dance floor, a little slower, a little more carefully. No trash talking now. I watch him whisper to his friends, sneaking a peek my way when he thinks I'm not looking.

The King slides down the bar and pulls off his shirt, wipes his mouth, then his nose, and tosses the crumpled, oily, rag at me.

"A time to love; a time for war." He pads to where the announcer is taking bets.

He's butchered it, but I don't correct him. No point. That's where his head's at right now: Love, war. I'm surprised he hasn't mutilated the verse further, added 'a time to eat' or something. I can see the mountain of wrappers, glistening under the bar lights. He's been inhaling them all day, recovering strength lost to that apparently insatiable worshiper.

Simon pulls up a chair and pours us both a glass of Yellow Label. It's no Maker's, which doesn't say much, but it's on the house and plentiful. "Is this going to be a David and Goliath sort of thing?"

"Doubt it."

He knows the score. "I hear Samson wanted to fight you instead. A cool thousand if you want to, win or lose."

"If he wins." I rub the spear tattoo that graces the inside of my right forearm. It itches. "But I'd probably kill him, and you'd be pissed."

"Hell no, he's a gladiator, a wolf, but it's time for some new blood around here. Do what you need to do."

"I doubt it will come to that." The bourbon goes down fast and I wonder, for a moment, if it's my cheeseburger, if I'm no different than my ward.

The long beard climbs up on his chair and hollers. The crowd, and it is a crowd tonight, quiets and makes some space for the two fighters. "Gentlemen. Lady folk. Tonight you're in fer a real treat. A contender has graced our blessed establishment. Fresh from taking down Joe, Caleb, and his brother Levi, give a loud welcome to the King."

Shouts. Fists pound tables. No slurs like last night, maybe even a bit of respect. The King grins his broken grin and scratches the long scar dominating his side.

"And defending his title of the last few months, give me a round for Samson, the Lion of Houma."

More cheering.

I take long sip and stand so I can see over the crowd, watch Samson pull off his wife beater. Muscles on muscles. His back dominated by a horse skull, lower jaw hanging askew. A monster, though no more than I am. There's more than a little kinship there. He pounds back a shot and tosses the glass into the crowd.

The King never hits first. That's not his way. He waits. He's patient. You'd expect him to be reckless, given his proclivity for impulsive eating and womanizing, but he isn't. Samson isn't either, he takes the King's measure, realizes immediately how it is, and starts with a hard left. Puts his weight into it. The King stumbles back into a chair, spraying blood. Sways. The crowd quiets, holds its collective breath.

But he gets up. Slides an arm across his dripping forehead, leaving a jagged crown shaped smear. I flashback to another place, another time, a day when he turned the other cheek and gave up. He's changed since then. Hardened. He'll never be that man again. I'm glad for it. For him. This time he has a choice, his own will, and uses it to give Samson a curt bow. An acknowledgement. Then goes on the offensive, a blur of jabs and punches. Forces the bigger man back.

It's clear the King's outmatched, but he doesn't quit. Not when he takes one in the gut so hard he pukes a bucket of burger puree. Not when he cracks an eye socket from a bludgeoning fist.

In the end, when Samson has the King up against the wall, putting in the finishing touches, the King whispers something in his ear, something too quiet for anyone else to hear. The big man stops, looks at the busted, bleeding out-of-towner like he's seeing him for the first time and blanches, paling under his mesh of tattoos and dark southern tan, before turning and walking away, through the crowd, right out the door.

Everyone glances around, not sure what's happened, if the fight is over. The din increases. People get fidgety. The announcer exchanges words with the judges, while a distinguished old gentleman, obviously a doctor, examines the King. Long story short, he's won it. Last man standing. Well, last man, anyways. The King slides into a chair and passes out while the doctor stitches him up and swaths his face in bandages.

Simon splashes down his drink and holds his glass up to the light. Twists it, watching the light blur through the ice. "Mighty strange, mighty strange..." He trails off, wondering, not sure what was whispered there, at the end.

I know, of course. What he said. What he always says.

🔥

"I forgive you," says the King, when I tell him I'd sent a limping and concerned MJ on her way while he slept like a baby. He doesn't, though, not really. Once he's up and about, woofing down the bag of cheeseburgers she left behind, he starts into it. "The earth trembled and quaked, the foundations of the heavens shook; they trembled because he was angry."

"Shut it. We've had this discussion before. You want to quote the scriptures? What about 'Do not spend your strength on women, your vigor on those who ruin kings.'"

"She is worth far more than rubies."

"Bullshit. This isn't even about her. You know that, so quit acting like I took away your new toy. I'm tired of it. All of it."

"You're tired? You have no—"

I cut him off. "I'm tired of watching you circle the drain, tearing yourself apart one bully and harlot and cheeseburger at a time. For what? They don't want to be saved. It's more obvious with every shit hole town we visit. And your strategy, if you can even call it that, is fucking terrible."

He rolls over on his bed, props himself up on an elbow, eyes squinting through gauze. "Yeah?

Then go. I never asked you to come, remember. You volunteered."

"You needed all the help you could get, and I thought you might have a chance this time. I was wrong. Open your eyes. Look at where we are." I gesture at the dirty beige carpet and tarnished gold wallpaper. "It's time to pack it in. Let it burn."

His eyes close and I see his jaw tighten. "No... There has to be something out there worth saving. I have faith."

There's a spark and I remember what's keeping me here. "Go take a shower, it's time to check out and be on our way. I found us a gig in Arkansas. A little town called Hope."

He gives me a tired look and struggles to his feet, still chewing. His bruises have faded, cuts sealing. Another scar or two to add to his collection, but he'll heal. He always does.

"I know, Gabriel, I know." The King holds up the now empty burger bag, presses it to his face and closes his eyes. Inhales, happy again. "I'll miss these, best I've had yet."

BANG.

He jumps as the door splinters apart and two men crowd in, firing AR-15's. I brush the shield tattoo on my left arm, but just for myself. They hose the room and the King, who's standing right in front of them, goes down in a fountain of blood and flesh, the bag fluttering to the floor. The single lamp explodes and the room goes dim, illuminated by what little dawn leaks through the shattered doorframe.

"Got you, you fucking terrorist asshole," one screams.

Even with their full body camouflage and black masks, I know them. Levi and Caleb. "Nice job, idiots." I heave myself off my chair, a bright spear appearing in my right hand.

They either don't see it or ignore it. "You're next, Arab lover."

Both brothers open up at close range and my shirt, a bespoke number from a little Garment District boutique I adore in Manhattan, shreds, and with it, the last of my patience. I retaliate with swift thrusts, ethereal flame sending two doomed souls down the express elevator to Hell.

The King is dead. Gross negligence at best and dereliction of duty at worst, but I need a break. It's not the first time, and not the last, and I'll deal with the inevitable consequences when they come due.

I'm still standing there, reflecting, when Simon shows up with two hatchet-faced men in black suits and takes in the King where he sprawls, perforated, the carpet drinking holy blood.

"Damn, sorry about that." He looks at me, jaw tight, the lines around his eyes deeper, darker. Exaggerated by my fading glow. "My men saw the brothers lurking in the parking lot. Figured they'd just put a couple shots in the window, give you a scare."

I shrug and step out of the darkness. They notice there's no blood, no wounds, see the shadow on the wall behind me, the glint on spear and silver-white feathers. All three take an involuntary step back but don't say a word. They're religious, god-fearing, but not good. Dark hearts. Hard souls.

"Shit happens," I say, breaking the spell.

Simon blinks away the vision and kicks Caleb, then Levi. "Idiots." He digs out a roll from his pocket, tosses it onto the bullet-mangled coffee table. "It's not much for a life, but take it with my apologies. Want to bury him? I can find space down at the church cemetery."

"Thanks, but I got this." I pull the sheet from his bed, drape it over the King, roll him up. As blood weeps, I rummage through my suitcase until I find a silver space blanket, the foil shroud crinkling like a giant burger wrapper. Simon and his men watch me slide him into our orange Subaru Outback, its darkly tinted windows folding around him like a tomb. Nobody says another word I as I toss in our suitcases and drive away.

It's six hours to Hope, but I can stretch it to three days of clean sheets, expensive bourbon, and some god damn peace and quiet.

PRODUCTION UPDATE #5

 **Terry (coordinator)**
April 1, 2022

The HPV is back, and it's not the nice kind everyone has and is cool with. Unfortunately it flares under stress. A pox on Gary is all I can say. It's been nearly impossible to work between tending the shrimp tanks, and visits to the clinic to get these growths lasered off. Especially when my Derm never misses an opportunity to fat-shame me. Yeah doc, I'm sure I wouldn't have bottomed for Gary in a desperate bid for validation and I magically wouldn't have caught his HPV if I'd only lost that last five hundred pounds. I'm asking for patience folks. We've got a new label printer and should be caught up very soon.

GLUTTONY

CAM HAYDEN

THERE WAS AN OLD LADY
BAP

URP!
GUH!
Bzzzzzzzzz
Bzzzzzzzzzz
Bzzzzzzzz
Bzzzzzz
Bzzzzzzzzzz
BZZZ
ZZZ
ZZ
Z
BZZNNNNNNNNN
ZZZ
GULP

BZZNK
SKITTER
SKITTER
SKITTER
EUGH!
GAK!
SKITTER
BOOSH!
SKITTER
SKITTER
SKITTER
SKITTER
SKITTER
SKITTER

KAK!
KAK!
SKITTER
SKITTER
SKITTER
SQUAWK!
GULP
HARD
DRY
SWALLOW
GARK!
SQUAWK!
SKITTER
CHOMP!

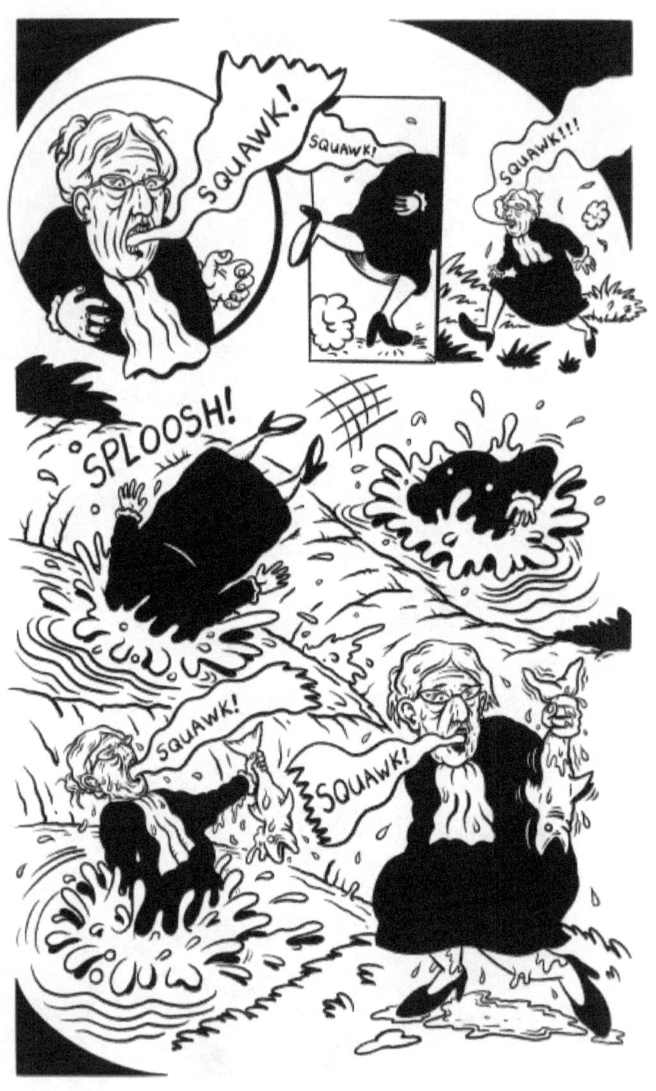
SQUAWK!
SQUAWK!
SQUAWK!!!
SPLOOSH!
SQUAWK!
SQUAWK!

SNIFF
SQUAWK!
SQUAWK!
WHUMP!
SQUAWK
MROWW!
SQUAWK!
SQUAWK!

SQUAWK
SQUAWK!
CRUNCH
SQUAWK!
SQUAWK!

SQUARK!
AWK!
AWK!
URK!
GURGLE
Cam Hayden
2020

PRODUCTION UPDATE #6

 **Terry (coordinator)**
July 4, 2022

I apologize for the long delay between updates. We've had a family emergency. My cousin ate a kid off the coast of New England. Just ate him! Twenty feet from the beach! We tried to talk some sense into her, to make her see that disordered eating is a serious problem. As Terrace rep for the Gluttons, I understand the urge to binge. Unfortunately she's now resting in pieces and my Aunt Karen is out for some great white revenge. But excellent news! After what seems like an eternal wait, books have arrived from the printer and let me tell you, they are exquisite! A welcome disgrace to any kitchen.

DEATH SHOT

KONN LAVERY

My hand shakes. The tip of the pen taps the paper, leaving marks of nervousness. Dot. Dot. Dot. I am to compose the most important message I will ever create. I don't write hand-written letters. The big boys upstairs must like keeping it old school. I'll play by their rules. After all, they'll determine the verdict of my soul. Here we go...

TO WHOM IT MAY CONCE—no, that's not personable enough... I know!

DEAR ANGEL OF DEATH, respectful, but too crude.

DEAR ARCHANGEL, there we go. Civil and direct.

A person can only make one first impression. I learned this from curating world-class art exhibits. If you walk with a little insecurity—BAM—you're pegged as prey, and the agent will walk all over you; stutter while making a deal, and you can forget about sticking to the budget. Seriously, it's a cutthroat industry. A hand-written letter is no different than a formal email or an alignment meeting—confidence, firmness, and clarity.

Yet, I am struggling, despite having done this a million times. I never thought I'd be making a case to justify my life, correction, my soul. I didn't believe in an afterlife because I'm practical. All of this is just wack. God, I wish I could get a line. Maybe I'll just ask the big man himself in a postscript: P.S. PLEASE PROVIDE ONE RAIL ON A GOLDEN TRAY.

The shock of rocking a coke binge, the Death Shot, a white light, and awakening here in the afterlife are on replay in my head, which is why I can't focus. The blinding light—what a cliché. Death is a big load to swallow.

"He's an archangel, right?" I shout through the crowded bar.

The round-faced man in front of me, puffing his cigar, takes it from his mouth and lets the smoke seep upwards. The century-old fashioned figure elegantly sips on his whiskey before answering, "haven't you ever read the scriptures, boy?"

My hand squeezes the pen. I am frustrated and weak. Why can't this guy throw me a bone? My question is a yes or no answer.

"I have," I finally say after a pause, sipping my whiskey.

"Then what would possess you to ask?" the man chuckles. "You know the answer."

"I want to make sure this is right!" I snap. "This Michael guy, he's the top dude to talk to?"

"Dude? Please. You vegetarians are all the same."

"I'm vegan, but that has nothing to do with this."

"Bushwa! It does," he points at me with his index finger. "Know your onions. Adolf Hitler was one of you."

"What? That's not the point. I just want to write this damn letter."

I feel agitation crawling up my back from attempting to talk to a man from over sixty years ago. Understanding his jargon isn't easy. Come to think of it, he is the only person I've seen from a different era. Everything here seems relatively modern, in a demented surreal way. Hell, I spotted a Starbucks when I first woke from the blinding light. Churchill must be in a culture shock. I want to ask him, but I don't see a point in doing so. He seems testy, as if there is a layer of desire hanging onto every word he speaks, like me.

He adjusts his bowtie and says, "it's not normal for a man to deny the animals God gave us."

I point upward. "Look how the good God treated us."

"You vegan-tarians are all wet, or whatever new terminology you came up with in the future. Or come up with, I should say." He smiles, knowing I am frustrated.

"It's just vegan," I mutter. "Look, that's got nothing to do with the letter. Should I address Michael?"

He leans back in his highchair, losing focus on me, gazing at the bar several tables away. His glass is still half full. He's distracted by two greasy suits in a heated discussion and a flirtatious couple whose hands can't wait to undress the other.

A young man behind the counter is wearing one of those high-class, five-star, top-dollar vested uniforms, all red and pinstriped. The only customization the bartender has is his pencil-thin wax-twirled mustache. One must wonder how long he spends each morning getting those curls just right. It makes me look like rubbish, waking up from OD'ing, hair every which way, and looking whiter than a corpse.

Woah. Glimmering emerald eyes pull me away from the exquisite bar. They belong to a pretty-pasty gal in a tight black dress, sitting alone. What a babe. I hadn't seen her when I first got here. I was probably in too much of a panic to notice. We lock gazes, and she doesn't blink.

One of the suits slams his fist, throwing me from the beauty-trance. He points aggressively at the other suit, raising his voice, which is muffled from the bar's noise. The look on his face says he is pissed.

I look back to the pretty-pasty girl. She is gone. Strange.

"My..." the man across from me says, licking his lips. "Say, whatever happened to that delicious bartender?"

"Sorry?" I say with agitation seeping from my voice. The speed of the conversation can't get to me. I'm impatient because I need to prove that I don't belong here—gluttony my ass. Tolerance and discipline are essential, just like any negotiation when I was alive. I can do this. Take it slow. Patience. I will get to write this letter.

"That bartender was an emotional rollercoaster. Loved it," the man says.

"I wouldn't know. I just got here, remember?"

"Oh, right. You're new. A future-man!"

I raise my hands, playing along. "That's right." Finding common ground is vital when you're in an alignment discussion. Like any art deal I've done, I'll relate to him. Hopefully, he buys it.

"You're too casual to write a letter of such importance," he says. "Do I have to remind you who you're talking to?"

"No, I know who you are," I rub my brow, wanting to get back to this stupid letter. My hand begins to shake. Yep, that is the withdrawal. As for the increasing weakness, I am not sure. Stress, I guess.

He puffs on his cigar and blows the smoke into my face, leaning closer on the round table. The candle in the middle emphasizes his wicked grin and the two sharp canine teeth. "Say it then."

"Winston Churchill," I say, not blinking through the cigar smoke.

My eyes begin to tear, but only a little. I remain cool because Churchill has the information I want. He knows it and isn't giving it up easily. As to why, who knows? Regardless, never did I think I would be sitting in a bar with one of the most significant figures in modern history.

He sits straight, puffing his chest, looking for a good ego suck. Time for me to get down on my knees, metaphorically. I won't blow him. That's not my thing. Well, maybe I would if it meant getting out of here. There's an exchange for the postscript: P.S. PLEASE PROVIDE ONE RAIL ON A GOLDEN TRAY, IN RETURN I'LL OFFER A BONE-LIPPING FOR THE BIG MAN.

"Sir Churchill," I say. "Is Archangel Michael the one I should be addressing the letter to?"

"Sure," Churchill says. His posture relaxes, seeming to approve of my newfound tone. "Or you could address God if you want."

"Right! He takes care of all souls, doesn't he?" Now there is traction. I can finally finish this introduction and start explaining my case.

"Let me ask you this. Do you think you're the first person to try writing to God for being wrongly accused?"

Churchill has a point. I wasn't anyone special on Earth. All I did was curate art. At the end of the day, when compared to all the souls in human history, one would say my contribution was pretty small. Then again, the people here seem to be around my time era, except for Churchill. He is the odd one out.

"The letter will get lost," I say, rubbing my nose. The frustration grows. I know I need a quick bump, just a small one. I'm a victim of jimmy-legs, and my brain feels squeezed dry. The motivation to talk lessens with each passing moment. Depression? No. It's like a lack of will to go on. It's got to be the realization that I'm in purgatory—such bullshit. A drug habit is no reason to judge someone's entire life's work unworthy.

Churchill licks his lips. "Yes, you're in such misery?"

I take a deep breath and manage to say, "no shit."

"No one wants to be down here, boy. No one believes that they would have to think about every little mistake they've made. Yet here you are, all twitchy. I've seen this behaviour before. The defeat. The desperation. The need."

"Fuck," I mutter to myself, fighting to gain strength.

Churchill licks his lips again, sweating like a pig. "I could sniff it a mile away. Delicious," he squeaks the last word.

That woke me up. "What?"

Churchill's tone returns to normal as he says, "you know who else was a drug addict?"

"Who?" I ask, humouring him.

"Adolf Hitler."

"Christ," I groan, leaning back in my chair.

"See? Vegan-tarians—all the same."

Again with the dietary choices! I lose my cool and shoot back, "oh yeah lard-ass, what about you? Let me guess, gluttony?"

Churchill puffs on his smoke. "That's not exactly relevant."

I look around the bar, eyeing the folks drinking and chatting. All of them fit in in terms of time. The hair and fashion match. "Okay, Man of Mystery, tell me why you are the only one that's ancient?"

"I beg your pardon?" Churchill asks.

"You called me 'future-man.' You're aware that you're the only person that isn't from your time, right?" I fold my arms, collecting my energy. Take that, withdrawal.

Churchill's eyes stray from the table, locking onto a couple of gals striding through the crowd. One is a cute little thing, crying with mascara running down her face. The taller friend holds her tightly. A slight grin forms on Churchill's face as he brings his cigar up for another puff. He's gone, sucked into the simple pleasures of man.

The women disappear into the crowd, and Churchill's trance ends with a jolt. He faces me, muttering, "tasty." He swirls his whisky and says, "listen, you seem to have it all figured out. I'm going to finish up and go back to my room. Have you seen the tellies we have?"

"You didn't tell me why you're here," I say.

Churchill downs the last of his whiskey. "No, I didn't." He stands, waving goodbye. "That's for me to know and you to guess."

"Hey," I say as he turns, walking away. "Hey!"

Nothing.

"Thanks for the drink," I say, taking a sip, defeated.

I got some info, at least. Churchill was the only one willing to talk to me in this damn bar. No one else gives a shit about my frustration. I suppose they see people dropping down from Earth all the time. Every wanker and his dog are in denial when finding out they are rejected from the good life post-death.

The intensity of my withdrawal lessens with each passing moment. I take a deep breath and have another drink of whiskey, collecting my thoughts.

"You should watch yourself," a silky voice says from behind me.

I look over my shoulder — nothing. I spin back to see that pretty-pasty gal walking over to the empty seat.

"May I?" she asks, gliding her elegant hand onto the wooden back. Her other hand has already placed her drink on the table.

"Be my guest," I reply, finishing the rest of my whiskey. "What'd you say?"

"You should watch yourself," she says, casually taking a seat, one arm on the chair. Her posture complements the confidence she has in that revealing dress. I like it.

"What makes you say that?"

"That isn't Churchill," she says.

"Who is it, then?" The words entice me, but I stay collected. I want to see what she is about first.

"His name is Mo," she says coldly.

"And who is this Mo guy?"

She takes a drink of her whiskey and says, "Motus 'Mo' Devoro. He's a demon, and he's hungry for misery."

"A demon?" My voice goes up, exposing my emotional responses. The news is jolting, even now, being among the dead. "I thought this was a place for people to redeem their sins?"

"It is, but angels and demons can come and visit. The afterlife is their domain, not ours."

"Huh, that explains why he's the only old-timer here. Everything else seems to be modern."

"You're quick."

"So, where is the real Churchill?

"He was here at one point. His time was up. Didn't you get the welcome package? It talked all about the famous residents."

I pat my pant pockets and check my leather coat. Nothing. "I must have lost it. This whole thing has been kind of a blur."

"I'd say. It happens to most newbies. I saw you stagger in here, all scared." She smirks. I think she likes me or wants something. I'll let this play out.

"And... Are you human?" I ask.

"Yeah. Don't worry. I'm not going to feed off you or anything."

"Feed?"

"Mo feeds off emotions, mostly negative ones. That's why he was so friendly to you. He does that to everyone who first comes here. He did it to me until I clued in."

"Wait? Is that why I feel so..."

"Weak? Like your will to go on is being sucked out of you?" She takes another drink.

"Yeah, that."

"Mo would be why. He's like an energy vampire. Ever hear of those?"

"Sort of. I thought that was all bogus."

"It is with humans, not with demons. Just stay away from Mo. He'll get nice and fat off you until you're dry as a raisin."

Well, that explains what 'Churchill' wanted. He was dangling a carrot, metaphorically, in front of me and gorging himself on my delicious misery. What a piece of shit. "No problem. So, does everyone know who he is?"

"Pretty much. Everyone gets a good laugh watching the newcomers get drawn into Mo's enchantment as he feasts off their sorrows."

"How nice of you all. You'd think he would pick a more realistic disguise."

"It worked on you, didn't it? The whole Churchill act? A recognizable figure, credible, he shouldn't exist. It's all masking the true bombastic character he is."

"That's predatorial."

"He'll treat you nice too, buy you a drink, hear your concerns, and even help you out a little. So be careful." She leans closer, clearly more interested in me. "What'cha working on anyways?"

I turn the letter over. The mystery of my note is the only thing I have over Pretty-pasty. I don't know who she is or what she wants. She could be using me too.

"I'm just writing. Mo gave me the paper and a pen."

"Let me guess, a letter to God?" she says, twirling her black hair.

She's good. I reply, "let me guess, you tried writing one to God too?"

"Can't say that I have. But others have. Want me to look it over?"

"I'm trying to figure out who I can address the letter to. I thought about the Archangel Michael."

"That's too high up. You'll never get his attention."

"Yeah, Mo said something similar," I scratch my nose. God, I need that bump.

She downs the rest of her whiskey in a single go. "How about I get us another?" she asks, eying my empty glass.

I now realize that my whiskey is gone from stress-guzzling. Another one would be nice, and so far, Pretty-pasty was good company and easy on the eyes. "Sure," I say.

Pretty-pasty gets up to fetch some drinks, leaving me with the letter, wondering who I should write this to. Maybe I can acknowledge someone further down the chain of command.

Heavy footsteps rise to my side. A deep raspy, "hey bud," follows, tingling my ear. The smell of smoke and dirt fill my nose. To my left, the sensations have derived from a hairy beast-of-a-man whose hand is large enough to crush my skull.

"Yeah?" I ask, feeling agitation from the revolving door of people coming to talk to me. What am I, an entertainment monkey?

"You lookin' a lil' desperate," he says.

"Who says that?"

"I got your snow."

My heart stops. Yes. The need. The desperation. Dealers sniff us out. Drug hounds go in for the kill. "How much?" I blurt out, not thinking about who this guy is, or remembering that the coke addiction got me in this mess. Even in purgatory, the temptation follows.

The man brushes his pointed goatee, saying, "cash doesn't work the same around here."

"What does?"

"Souls."

Wait a minute, that's a ghastly currency! "Are you some demon?" I ask.

Before the man can answer, Pretty-pasty grabs a couple of drinks from the bar and starts making her way back.

"Think about it," the drug hound says, pushing a small note against my elbow. The scent of smoke fades as the heavy footsteps dissipate from the white noise of the bar.

I look at the note, seeing it is a room number, "Suite 66".

Pretty-pasty arrives, sliding the glass over.

"Thanks," I stare at the whiskey, judging it. Souls are required for coke. A demon feeds off emotions. What does Pretty-pasty want? "Is everyone here preying on newcomers?" I ask.

"Everyone? No. You just walked into one of the more immoral bars."

"Great. And how do I know you're not a parasite too?"

Pretty-pasty raises her glass. "That's a risk you're going to have to take." She has a drink, not losing eye contact.

Pretty-pasty is right. I don't have any allies. Hopefully, I don't need to make any, and I can get out of here. For now, Pretty-pasty doesn't seem threatening. She's what I'd consider a low-risk interaction, which is a colleague you can use down the road. It's a tactic I mastered in the art of negotiation. Maybe I can leverage her if I need help.

Pretty-pasty points her index finger at the note, "you should probably address that to Michael's executive assistant."

"Yeah?" Alright! Pretty-pasty proves useful. "What's their name?"

"Bonni."

I take a quick sip of my drink, flipping the paper over and jot down, DEAR EXECUTIVE ASSISTANT BONNI. Bingo.

"What's the address to Heaven?" I ask.

Pretty-pasty almost snorts out her whiskey. "Cute," she sputters.

"Seriously."

"Just put Heaven."

"Think that's good enough?"

"Honestly, I have no idea. I haven't heard of anyone who has successfully written a silly letter to redeem their sins."

Great. A blast of defeat scorches me. Her words are discouraging. Yet, I know damn well that I don't belong at Purgatory Towers. Drugs aren't like consuming food or wealth, and I keep thin because of my veganism lifestyle and not the coke. I can elaborate on the vegan life in the letter. That's got to be worth some points. Worst case, if it fails, I can track down that drug hound and get some snow. If I'm destined to be down here, why not? In fact, I could even use a bump just to power through this letter and end my jimmy legs. They haven't stopped bouncing.

Pretty-pasty's eyes widen. "God, you're bleeding," she says, leaning over to me.

A droplet of red falls on the table, coming from my nose. I touch my nostril, feeling more blood.

Pretty-pasty pulls out a handkerchief from inside her bra and leans over the table, dabbing my upper lip and nose with the warm cloth. She keeps pressure on my face for several moments. I can't see her eyes over the handkerchief, so I stare at her cleavage. The view isn't bad.

"Thanks," I say nasally.

"Don't worry about it. Look, you might have been some hotshot amongst the living, but down here, you're a newbie. Take it down a notch and ride out your punishment. Plus, it isn't so bad, we all have a subscription to Factory Prime. You can stream whatever you want and there's next-day delivery."

I presume she meant some video streaming service. I say, "and just stare at a T.V. screen, waiting for our time to end?"

"Not quite. You need to work still. I'm at the Factory, most people are. The work is labour intensive, and the tentacles are weird, but you get great discounts."

"Are you trying to recruit me?" I ask.

"No, trust me. I'm just letting you know how it works."

"And why is that?" I ask.

She looks to the ground, biting her lip. She's nervous. The moment passes, and she stares at me with those hypnotic eyes. "Let's just say friends are a rare thing around here."

There we go. Pretty-pasty is lonely. A simple concept I didn't even fathom. There must be all sorts of creeps in purgatory. She thinks I'm a decent guy and decided to take a risk talking to me, as I am her. She longs for something pure, and all I want is pure cocaine and a ticket out of here. Interesting. I'll keep this tidbit of information in my toolkit.

"But why not humour you?" Pretty-pasty checks the handkerchief for more blood and deems me cured of the nosebleed. She jumps off her stool and scoots it closer to me. Her molasses smell compliments her good looks. "Let's see what you got."

No longer worried, I pass her the paper. "I only have the first line," I say, taking a drink and scanning the rest of the bar.

I can't get that drug hound out of my mind. He has coke, and I need to lose this withdrawal to think clearly. One bump would fix it. Most of the shakes and sweat are gone, but I know it will be back. Times of stress doesn't help either. I can barely think, thanks to the withdrawal and this afterlife nonsense. A small line would get me right.

The drug hound. Souls. Coke. Pretty-pasty. Trust. My scheming mind is brewing up a vindictive plan, one that I am not proud of, and I feel rotten just thinking about it. Unfortunately, I am good at shifting people around and stepping on them, which my assistant was all too familiar with. Using folks isn't a skill to be proud of, but you know, it gets the job done.

Plus, these damn jimmy-legs. Oh great, the sweat is coming back. Hey, Pretty-pasty has a cute dimple, I didn't see that before. Okay, no. I'll push the moral concerns aside and run this plan through. That doesn't mean I'll go through with it, it's just an idea. The plan is something like this: the drug hound has coke in exchange for souls. I probably want to keep mine and can charm Pretty-pasty into befriending me. Then, I can sell her off and see how much coke that gets me after we write this letter. Wait, no, thinking it through makes me sound awful. I'm talking about selling someone's soul. That's evil with a capital 'E.' I don't even know how to sell a soul for some coke. I can't... or can I? Pretty-pasty is just some bar trash, right?

The diabolical plan spins in my head the more Pretty-pasty and I chat. My pocket houses the drug hound's note, continually reminding me that coke is only a soul away. Morality is eating away at me. Then, moments go by where I forget about the plan. Pretty-pasty and I laugh. I tell her about the crazy agents and painters I dealt with while alive. We exchanged names. Truthfully, I can't remember hers. Something about 'Pretty-pasty' sticks. Plus, I'm too focused on making her laugh with my life stories, and my own needs.

She is smiling and asks me why I think I was wrongfully accused. I tell her straight up, "I had a bad cocaine habit."

"Had or have?" she asks, still smiling.

"Have, I suppose."

"I'm going to guess that's how you died too?"

"Half right."

"Oh?"

"Yeah, I was at an afterparty from an opening for Oscar Elvira."

"Wait, the Oscar Elvira?" Pretty-pasty asks.

"Yeah, you know him?"

"Of course, I love his contemporary work! Some of his post-modern futurism stuff didn't live up to his quality, you know?" Pretty-pasty sounds genuinely excited. Cute, passionate, and a great taste in art. This isn't helping my dilemma.

I clear my throat, keeping calm. "Totally. So, I was schmoozing it up with a couple of big agents from France. It turns out they were coke fiends too. My assistant, Clark, and another artist joined us in their executive suite hotel room. One of these France guys pulls out a nasal spray — cleverly disguising liquid cocaine. He asks if we'd ever done a Point-Blank."

"What's that?"

"Well, it's supposed to be like a Kamikaze shot but with a drop of coke."

"Sounds intense."

"It's not really if you're into the drug. Taking it orally doesn't hit you the same. Anyways, we all did a Point-Blank, a couple of rails, more liquor, and kept living the party life. Later, the time came for some more Point-Blanks. The French agent brings out a bigger bottle of clear liquid. Man, I had no idea where they got all this coke. We were thrilled and decided to use bigger glasses, like eight ounces big."

"Woah," Pretty-pasty says, clearly impressed by how I partied. She must be of the same life.

"But I needed a smoke. Foolishly I left to the balcony, letting my guard down, thinking they'd just pour another Point-Blank."

Pretty-pasty plays with her hair saying, "big shot art dealer, the master of people-skills, let his guard down?"

"Shut up, we all did that night. One of the agents joined me outside while the artist went for a piss. The other agent and Clark were pouring the shots. I don't know what happened in that kitchen, but Clark had been trying to undermine me for months."

"You think he poisoned you?"

"He gave me liquid cocaine. He wants my job and probably got it by making an expensive deal with that agent. Coke isn't cheap. We all gathered in the kitchen, cheered, and downed our Point-Blanks in one go. Instantly I knew that shot wasn't a Point-Blank. That was a damn Death Shot. A one-way ticket to Hell."

"Purgatory."

"Whatever."

Pretty-pasty gently touches my arm. "Sorry, newbie."

"I wish I could just beat the living shit out of Clark."

"That would be wrath. Then you'd have no chances of getting into Heaven."

"Right," I say, staring down at the paper.

Pretty-pasty says, "now that I know how you died and about your coke addiction, maybe we can spin that in your letter. Shall we?"

"I'm vegan."

"Okay?"

"I do good things! Coke is just a party supply."

"Alright, Mr. High Ground," she says, grabbing the pen.

We start writing. Time is a blur. Pretty-pasty brings us more drinks as the barflies dwindle. The two of us are some of the last folks here. We're pretty piss-faced, which only fuels the itch for coke. Great. At some point I took the pen back and wrote the last few words.

"Done," I say, my legs are still bouncing up and down.

"Woohoo!" Pretty-pasty says as we clang glasses.

The letter is a beauty. Drunkenness aside, I am sure of it. We even elaborated on my ethical eating choices and how it helps the planet.

Proving I have done an unmeasurable amount of good by saving animals. "Glad you came around," I say. Regret starts to clog my throat. I'm not sure if I can even go through with selling her off for some blow. I still don't know who she is. But the itch... it's getting worse with each drink.

"Say, why are you here?" I ask.

"Me?" Pretty-pasty says, blushing. "I made some bad choices."

"Seems pretty human."

The bartender shouts that they're closing up. It's now or never. I could either fumble around and try to make it another day in purgatory, mail my letter, and wait. Or, I can get some snow, get that last fix, and mail out the letter. If this letter works—and it's a damn good letter—I won't be hanging around here with Pretty-pasty anymore. If it doesn't... well, I know where I can get coke again.

I clear my throat, pushing doubt down. "Hey, listen. Do you want to come back to my place? I haven't exactly been there." I pull out the note from my pocket to show her. "I kind of ran into this bar in a panic when I arrived."

"You did," she slurs, taking the note. "You wrote your address down but lost the welcome package?" She raises her thin brow. We enter a stare-down duel of trust. Did I fuck up? Moments pass.

She snorts. "You're so stupid."

The victor: me. I shrug smoothly. "Hey, I'm a newbie. So, where is that exactly?

"I'll show you if you'd like?" Her voice is tender while passing me the note. If only I could have both the blow and the girl.

"Yeah," I say, staying cool.

"It's on the sixth floor," she says, hopping off her stool with a slight tumble. She doesn't look embarrassed and recovers. "I'm good."

"You sure?" I smile. Oh no, I'm liking Pretty-pasty. Now I'm unsure if I can even go through with this. The sad part is, I actually did lose that welcome package that had my number and key.

Pretty-pasty and I leave the bar in a drunken swagger, arm-in-arm. She is proving to be the kind of girl I would have hung out with when I was alive, maybe even girlfriend material. Then my nose itches and a cold sweat brews. Of course, when I start to experience reason, the desire creeps back up into overbearing demand.

I'm a chained slave to the drug, being pulled into the darkness once again. It doesn't help that Pretty-pasty is leading me right to that temptation with no knowledge of it. I could come clean. I could.

We walk out of the bar and into the outlandish winding halls, covered in bastardized religious symbols and otherworldly wiggling appendages. Animated paintings... or ghosts and breathing rugs, are they alive? With so much to see, I lose my train of thought and am barely able to keep track of where Pretty-pasty is taking me—a turn here, and a staircase there. Next thing I know, we are at a red door with golden letters 66 nailed to it. This is it. She turns to me.

"Well?" Pretty-pasty says. "You got your key?"

"I... uh..." Shit, I didn't think this far. Instincts kick in, and I boldly grab the doorknob. It twists, and to my luck, the door opens.

"You sure this is your place?" she asks, following me inside the dark room.

"Yeah, of course," I lie. "I just lost the welcome package."

A spotlight beams down on a black table with a golden tray, housing a mound of cocaine. Hot damn. There is no furniture or decorations, only an open space that leads into blackness. The door slams shut, and we both cower. Pretty-pasty, visibly shaken, backs up into me. I grab her. By the door, the drug hound stands, all hairy and smoky.

"So, you do want some snow after all?" he says with a toothy grin, revealing his fangs.

"Yeah," I say, thinking that Pretty-pasty would start to freak out now. She looks worried, almost confused by everything. Maybe she is more desperate and drunk for friendship than I thought. Now I feel even worse.

"Good," the drug hound says. He points to Pretty-pasty. "Yours?"

"No." I let go of Pretty-pasty. "The—" I choke from the swelling guilt pushing back up into my throat. I don't think I can even finish my sentence.

Pretty-pasty is looking at the drug hound and me, back and forth, several times.

No, this isn't right. I can't. "I—" my words are cut short by Pretty-pasty.

"Wait. You asshole, were you going to sell me off?" She pushes me hard, and I manage to keep my intoxicated balance.

"No, wait," I say, trying to justify my remorseful actions.

"That's not a surprise," the drug hound says. "From a vegan-tarian."

"What?" I say.

The drug hound's body bubbles. Bones crack. The flesh rips, moving and fusing anew as the skin colour morphs. His whole form warps into the indistinguishable Winston Churchill, better known here as Motus "Mo" Devoro. Hell, even his clothes mutate too, like some sort of magic act. That cunning prick, of course, there is shapeshifting. I'm out of here.

I stomp towards the door and Mo.

"Leaving so soon?" Mo says, licking his lips. "Already I can sense the frustration in you... the emotion. You're so close to what you need, are you not?"

I look over my shoulder to see the pile of cocaine, then Pretty-pasty, who held her one arm, looking at Mo intently.

"You coming?" I ask her.

"Eat a dick," Pretty-pasty hisses with a pink face. She's pissed. I'm messing this up. Maybe if I get us out, she'll come around.

Mo stands closer to the door. "No one is leaving until a deal is made."

"Says who? Nothing is binding us," I say. "No deal."

Mo laughs. "What makes you think something needs binding?"

"I don't know. What about those contracts and deals with the devil?"

"You mean in Hollywood?" Pretty-pasty shakes her head. "You are such a newbie. Mo isn't going to let us leave."

I scratch the back of my neck, looking at the pile of coke and then Mo, who is grinning, showing off his two sharp teeth.

"So, how does this work?" I ask, folding my arms.

"Well," Mo says. "It's quite the scene. First, we need to tie her down and carve a plethora of demonic symbols into her flesh. Then, I cut my hand, raining blood down on her, fusing her to me."

"That sounds horrible!" I say.

"It's either you or her," Mo says. "I'm not letting you both leave. But I am a fair dealer. I give in return."

Pretty-pasty and I lock eyes. She is furious. That scowl. My guilt.

The victor: Pretty-pasty. I can't go through with this. There must be a way out of here, for both of us. I need to think. The drunkenness is making me slow. I need that bump. Wait a minute. Yes. The scheming mind is doing its work.

"How do I know this is real coke?" I ask.

"Fair question," Mo says, gesturing to the pile. "Give it a try. My goods are top shelf."

Fool. I'll feed this fixation and get my brain firing on all cylinders. I've pulled off crazy deals in the past after a quick one. I wink at Pretty-pasty while walking over to the golden tray, hoping she trusts me.

My eyes widen while walking. There must be about a quarter of a million bucks sitting on this table, the equivalent of a soul. Wow. I've never seen this much at once.

Mo takes a deep satisfying breath. "My, my, so much pent up excitement from you both. Please, embrace a line. We'll get to business after."

Gross. As I get my fix, old Mo here is sucking off my energy like a baby on a tit. I can feel his misery-slurping lingering in my body. It's weakening me. I push the sensations aside, realizing I need to stay focused. Without hesitation, I snag my hand-written letter from my pocket and roll it into a beautiful thin tube as I section off a fatty with the note.

Sorry big boys upstairs, down I go on the white road with one big SNIFF. God yes! I missed that. Who knew purgatory would have access to such greatness? This is good stuff. Almost too good. Another rail wouldn't hurt. I line it up and take another loud SNIFF. Wow. The drunken slur is fading fast. A familiar buzz hums through my veins, nurturing my poor malnourished addiction. Come on, brain, start scheming a way out.

"And done!" Mo says with excitement. "Pleasure doing business."

I spin around, bug-eyed, with white powder all over my nostril. "We haven't started the deal!" I snap.

"Pleasure was all mine, asshole," Pretty-pasty says.

"What?" I say, flabbergasted, realizing Mo wasn't talking to me.

Mo has a one-page document in his hand with a red splotch on it, right beside a black signature. Pretty-pasty is holding onto a pen and that bloody handkerchief in the other. Mo is breathing heavily as sweat drips onto the floor. My heart rate is increasing from the drugs and boiling fear. That paper... the blood. Did they just?

"Wait. What? The note..." Words aren't coming quickly like they usually do with coke. I'm stifle with disbelief. Mo and Pretty-pasty lied to me. Selling a soul is like in the movies. A simple contract binds it with blood. I am the fool who was so desperate to get that bump. I wonder if Pretty-pasty was planning this from the beginning. She was so genuine, like she really needed to connect with someone. But who has handkerchiefs stuffed in their bra? Plus, she approached me, like Mo did. It doesn't matter now.

Pretty pasty narrows her eyes, saying, "still think your letter is going to do you any good? Being bound to a demon?"

"Fuck you!" I shout, not buying into what just happened. "I'm out of here." This can't be real. I take my first step to the door, yet my legs reject my instructions, as I stare at the doorknob that is too far from reach. No. My legs... don't listen to me. I snag one, trying to lift it with all my might. Nothing.

Mo holds out his hand. "It doesn't quite work that way."

I don't know what to say and just stare at my leg with intense crushing tunnel vision, thanks to the coke buzzing through my mind.

"You're my tasty little treat!" Mo squeaks, walking towards me. "Your anger, oh my! So succulent."

Pretty-pasty twists the handle on the door.

I shoot back to reality and yell before she leaves. "Hey, lady! Do you think God is going to let you go into Heaven after this? You're stuck down here with the rest of us."

She looks at me with those magnetic eyes, saying, "I knew that about me long before you arrived."

"I was going to get us both out."

"No, you weren't," Pretty-pasty says. "I know addicts, no matter how cute they are."

"Fuck you," I say through my teeth.

"You asked what I did to get here?"

"I don't care," I say.

"I did this kind of thing, any deal to take a shortcut."

"So, it all worked out great for you," I say.

"I guess so. No more Factory work after selling a fresh soul. Sorry newbie." Her lips press tightly while stepping out into the hall, leaving me alone with Mo.

Mo's skin is so moist as he downs his good misery-stake. "Oh yes, we'll keep this lovely feast rolling. You'll be a shrivelled up little prune," he says.

My heart continues to pound, punching against my ribcage. The drugs melt into the fear, the anger, and the desperation, creating a boiling stew of raw human energy. The kind of dessert a demon of the afterlife would love. Will I live? Will I die in purgatory with Mo feasting off every drop of life I have? What happens then? Questions swirl around my mind a million miles a minute.

The demon is turning red as two horns erect from the top of his head. His body slowly morphs into a demonic version of the drug hound, presumably his natural form. I swear that tub is getting fatter the longer I stand here, withering away to an almost mummified state. I feel so dry.

Then, those advantageous two rails provide me with one last buzz of brilliance. Yes... oh yes. That resourceful mind is doing what it does best. I can escape Mo's feeding. That soul contract might be trickier. I never did get to read the fine print. This plan better work.

Mo is close to me, moaning, getting his fill of the energy buffet for one. My body is weak, and my legs aren't responding, but my upper half is. The mound of cocaine is so close. The temptation that offed me, prevented me from getting into Heaven, and locked my soul into a dance with a demon, is now the key out of here.

I'm still by the table, and I loosen my grip on the letter, widening the circumference, and exhale slowly, removing all oxygen. Ready. The demon's yellow eyes slowly open as I calm my emotions, watching as I bring the paper to my nostril. Mo gasps as I divebomb into the mound of white benevolence. The powder flies up the vast chamber, through the nasal cavity, and blitzes my brain with exemption pearls.

"Wait!" Mo shouts, spit flying from his mouth. "No!"

The demon's food-spell ends, and he raises his claws upward. My arm freezes, his power over my soul locking my limbs and spine first. My breathing begins to whither as I suck in every bit of coke I can, lungs stretching beyond capacity as Mo shuts them down.

Come on white mountain! Those little shards of mercy are running rampant inside my bloodstream. Mo has locked my whole body.

How long have I been frozen now? The ghost of the Death Shot haunts me, with a familiar yet overbearing sensation I once feared: dying. Yes... I remember... I see... numbness. The cliché blinding light!

PRODUCTION

UPDATE #7

 Terry (coordinator)
August 18, 2022

The hagfish is back. I suspect she never left. Our books are destroyed, the entire print run utterly slimed. My gods, my gods, why have you forsaken me?

FML…

TUNY

JULIE HINER

Petunia Price cranked her neck up one notch at a time. Her gaze lingered on the mirror's border, ornate golden curls, like the last design she'd created with her Spirograph. She slammed her eyes shut, willing little threads to stitch themselves over her eyelids, so she'd never have to look at herself again. *Tuny, stop being a baby.* She hung her head and stared at her feet. Red shag carpet tickled her toes as she wiggled them. *All right, Tuny,* she coaxed herself in her mother's voice. *You need to look.*

Heat pulsed through her meaty cheeks. She squeezed her eyes tight, swallowed hard, then snapped her eyelids open. Full-length mirror, it was supposed to be. It was, for *normal* teenagers. Her dwarfish stature barely covered half the length of the glass. Her vertical growth had halted a long time ago. She could not, however, see the outline of her stomach. It bulged way past the sides of the mirror. She could only take in her full girth by spinning like a porcelain doll perched on a stand. *Stupid dress.*

She'd begged her mom to buy it for her. It was the prettiest thing she'd ever seen, hanging from the perfect body of the mannequin. Tingles of delight had burst through her when she discovered the dress laid out on her bed. Until she saw the tag. Until she saw the size. *'It's not as tight as you think. Just cut back on those treats.'* Her mother's taunting voice seared her ears. Her puffy marshmallow figure looked ridiculous stuffed into light blue lace. The unbreathable material cooked her in the rancid juices secreting from her pores. Heat swelled around her thick neck as sweat pooled in the fleshy folds of her stomach.

She stared at the blue beluga in front of her eyes. A reflection shimmered across the glass. A flash, a glimmer of a girl that was there for an instant then gone the next. An image of the girl she desired to be. The girl that appeared between binges. Did this girl exist? A gurgle erupted from her stomach.

She stared again at the fat sausage stuffed into a casing two sizes too small. She knew the truth. She saw the rolls of flesh bulging against her thin, stupid dress.

Hot tears melted into her cheeks.

Spit flew from her mouth as she yelled at the girl in the mirror. "Stupid, fat Tuny!"

She longed to peel off her skin and walk out of it. It felt foreign, wrong, like a forced costume. *'You look pretty, Tuny.'* Her mother's voice coaxed. *'You'd be prettier without your treats.'*

Stupid dress.

The room spun, whirling blue lace, golden curls and red shag into a smear of cosmic colour. Her knees buckled. The weight of her elephant body sunk into the soft shag. She crumpled into a ball. Bile crawled up her throat. She clamped her eyelids together, picturing the one thing that would calm her. She wanted to resist. To learn from the hell she continually created for herself. The thought of chocolate and caramel teased her.

A loud sigh seeped from her lips. She turned toward the bed and crawled on all fours like a wiener dog wading through red grass. Lifting the bed skirt, she reached underneath.

Her fingers squirmed through the carpet. *Where is it?* Panic shot through her insides. She grasped at empty air with her pudgy fingers.

I didn't eat them all. Her fingers grabbed at nothing. Pain sliced her shoulder as she slammed it against the bed frame, smashing her squishy cheek into the mattress. She reached her stubby arm as far as she could.

I didn't eat them all. Sweat soaked her back, drenching the blue lace. Her stomach swirled. She gagged.

No! I didn't eat them all. She probed farther. Her pinky finger hit the corner of a box. She grabbed until she found a good grip. Pulling it through the carpet jungle, the contents rattled against the cardboard. *Tat-tat-a-tat.*

Sitting back on her heels, she slid the top off the box and stared at the half-empty tray of shiny, turtle-shaped chocolates, gooey caramel seeping from their sides, nuts dotting their shiny brown backs.

Petunia grabbed a chocolate so hard her fingers sunk into its dark shell. She shoved it into her mouth, all of it. Vigorous chomping followed. Chocolate-caramel sludge seeped from the corners of her mouth. She sunk her ample pillow bum into the rug, stretching her plump legs in front of her, head spinning in candy-coated glee.

As the sweet glop oozed down her throat, her stomach settled, and calm washed over her. As soon as the sucrose high teetered toward the tail end, another revolt rumbled inside her. She grabbed another chocolate and shoved it in her mouth.

The mashed-to-pulp turtle slid down, clinging to the sides of her throat.

Puff. Her stomach pushed against the lace. Plunging turtle number three into her waiting mouth, she devoured it with more vigour than the first two.

Gulp. Slide. *Puff.* The blue lace protruded out another notch. Turtle four didn't stand a chance.

Gulp. Slide. *Puff. Puff.* The blue lace stretched over her ballooning stomach. Turtle five met his death. Six barely got a chance to breathe. Seven was never seen again.

Gulp. Gulp. Gulp. A series of chocolate reptiles sliding to a bottomless pit. *Puff. Puff. Puff.*

Tuny looked down at the box in dismay. How is it empty? She only opened it that morning. Humph. She grunted as she rolled onto her knees and rose to her feet. Shuffling back to the mirror, she stared at a pale blue whale smeared in shit.

She didn't care. Her mind twirled glucose-fuelled pirouettes.

A gurgle erupted in her stomach. She looked at her bloated middle. I'm starving. *Why is dinner taking so long?*

In a flash she remembered hot vomit spewing from her mouth, the cold porcelain bruising her chest. *No, that won't happen this time.* She needed more food. Now.

She cracked open her bedroom door and peered down the hallway like a robber. Nothing. No movement. No noise.

She tiptoed down the hallway toward the smell of roasting meat wafting from the kitchen. Laughter drifted up the stairs, from the basement. They were all down there, occupied with their traditional Thanksgiving Day movie fest. They thought she was taking a nap.

Walking like a ballerina, she approached the oven. The cooking flesh tickled her nostrils. Her mom's floral-patterned oven mitts sat on the counter. She picked them up and slid them over her hands. She opened the oven. Golden, crispy skin encased a juicy turkey. It looked ready. Tuny looked at the clock on the stove. Four o'clock. Plenty of time before the clan clambered up the stairs.

Would the flesh inside the beast be cooked to the required safe temperature? *Did it matter?*

Tuny pulled the oven door all the way down. Clouds of steam hit her face. She ignored the wet heat and the burnt smell as she plunged her head right into the oven. She pulled the rack with her gloved hand until the turkey perched in front of her. Kneeling on her puffy knees, she ripped off the mitts and threw them onto the cracked linoleum.

Tuny dug her hand into the crevice of the body. Stuffing singed her fingers. Pain seared through her arm. She dug further, only retracting her hand when she had an ample handful of spiced bread.

She shoved the handful into her mouth. The insides of her cheeks screamed against the heat. The buttery cubes melted in her mouth, slid down her throat and coated her stomach. Her mind fuzzy, she floated into butter-dough bliss. She plunged her bright-red hand into the body of the beast again. With every bite, the lace around her growing stomach expanded and stretched. *Chew, swallow, puff.*

The bird was empty.

Without hesitation, she ripped a leg from the carcass. Grease drizzled down the corners of her mouth as she devoured the dark flesh. *Chew, swallow, puff.* Small tears ripped through the lace around the heart of her belly. Both legs gnawed to the bone, her fingers plunged into the browned breast. *Chew, swallow, puff, puff.* Fissures erupted through the pretty lace. Her arms and legs swelled along with her protruding belly.

Bones piled around her on the floor, pieces of leg, breast, and thigh clinging to her hair, her dress, and her skin. The carcass sat bare in the roasting pan. Tiny shreds of meat clung to the neck of the bird. She ripped it from the body and chewed it clean.

Tuny look around her. She slumped into a crumpled heap of fat. *How had this happened?* She swallowed hard against the dread crawling up her throat. *Could she stop?* She closed her eyes and tilted her head back. Saliva swam around the back of her tongue as fresh baked pastry and sweet fruit taunted her nostrils. *Where was it coming from?*

She waddled to the countertop, seeking her next prey.

She had to keep going. She couldn't face that cold plummet down the dark shaft to the bottom of the glutton well. As long as she kept her mind buzzed with butter and grease, she wouldn't have to.

Her mom's pumpkin pie sat near the window, waiting. Tuny fumbled at the pie, pulling it across the countertop toward her waiting mouth. Her fingers sunk into the soft pumpkin puree. Scoop after scoop, the candied pumpkin slid down to her stomach.

Suck, swallow, puff, puff, puff. Her grannie panties split down the seam. The lace scraped against her dough skin. Lost in the crumbling pastry dream, she didn't notice. Scooping the last handful into her open mouth, she gaped at the empty pie plate. *Where did it all go?*

She scanned the counter in a frantic burst of search and destroy. Passing over items that were a waste of time—salad, carrots, brussels sprouts—her eyes found their target. A loaf of freshly baked bread. She penguin shuffled over to the bread. She picked it up in both hands and broke it open. Shoving half the loaf into her mouth, gasping for air as she swallowed, the massive chunks caught in her throat.

A tiny voice inside of her screamed for help. It was muffled, then silenced by pieces of bread tumbling into her stomach. *Shovel, swallow, puff, puff, puff, puff.* The cracks in the blue lace ruptured into crevices over her belly, back, and butt. The dress could no longer hold her bulging being. Pain carved across her stomach.

'*Tuny. Stop.*' Her mother's face loomed. '*You look pretty.*' her mother pleaded. '*No more treats.*' Her mother, telling her not to eat, even while shoveling the last Ding Dong from a freshly opened package into her own mouth. '*Don't eat, Tuny,*' her mother snarled at her between savage bites of chocolate cake, saliva drenched whipped cream dripping from her chin.

Eat. Don't eat. Pretty dress. Too tight. Tuny's mind whirled.

Shut up. Eat.

Her throat dry against the chunks of bread, she shovelled the other half of the loaf into her mouth in massive morsels. *Shovel, shovel, swallow, gulp, puff, puff, puff. Riiip.*

Skin split from neck to navel.

Her insides exploded with the release of pressure. Greasy Tuny meat soared across the kitchen in all directions, splatting against the old stove, the puke-green counter, and the cracked cupboards. A glob of flesh clung to the canister holding the shiny silver serving spoons. Chunks of Tuny slid down the cupboards, leaving bloody smears like an abstract painting.

As pieces of her rained through the air, Tuny had a last moment of conscious thought. Her mind was clear. She could see the truth. Staring at herself in the full-length mirror back in her bedroom, red shag carpet tickling her toes, she looked into her own eyes, seeing herself for the first time. A girl in blue lace dress. Normal. And pretty.

PRODUCTION

UPDATE #8

 **Gary (manager)**
December 21, 2022

Dearest backers,

Thank you for your patience. The books and applicable rewards have shipped with individual tracking numbers sent out via email.

And for the record, I don't know where Terry got that particularly demonic HPV from, but it wasn't me.

GRAVESEND

SARAH L. JOHNSON & ROBERT BOSE

The odd clap of a hardcover, cleared throat, or mobile ding banged off the skylights of the Edwardian library in Gravesend. Any silence between filled by the relentless keyboard clack of the Kidz Coding Club beneath the mezzanine where Sol and Trace sat with a distraught Ms. Lydia Winsett.

"Hate to break it to you, sweetheart, but there's no such thing as leprechauns," said Sol, tossing a handful of roasted peanuts into his mouth.

Lydia dropped her puffy face into her hands and began to sob. Then she began to wail. Trace kicked Sol under the table. "Aren't you supposed to be the romantic one?" She wrapped her arms around the bawling lady. "Uh…Lydia, we're getting a few looks here, so maybe blow your nose and keep it down, yeah?"

Sol folded his scarred arms across his chest, chewing peanuts to butter and dying for a smoke. "So what, this guy did a runner on you?"

"He said the stories were all true," Lydia honked into an honest to god lace-trimmed hankie, gesturing to the reference section, its rows of shelves crammed with decaying volumes of local history, myth, and lore. "He said he'd been waiting, for someone like me, all his life."

"A librarian?" Trace cocked her head.

Lydia sniffed. "I knew he couldn't be human, the way he touched me, he had this power… I couldn't get enough. We made love in the stacks, in the accessibility elevator. The rare book room. In…" She flailed an arm at Sol. "That chair."

The desecrated chair screeched as Sol shot to his feet, spraying peanuts across the table.

Trace cringed as Lydia snuffled into her shoulder. "Aside from slicking every surface of your work in DNA and pulling an Irish Houdini, what's the story?"

"This isn't our kind of business," Sol said, still standing awkwardly over the table. Goddamnit, this was supposed to be a vacation. Or at least a couple weeks to lay low and not actually look for trouble. Too bad Trace was a workaholic. "Ms. Winsett, I don't think we can help you."

Lydia's soft brown eyes locked with his. "Yuvrani Kaur said this was exactly your kind of business."

"Damn her and her big mouth," Trace swore.

Sol groaned. They were lucky to have a few friends in various corners of nowhere and Yuvrani had offered discreet accommodation at the Sikh temple in Gravesend where she served as Granthi. All because Trace insisted they make a trip to the U.K. *"A vacation,"* she'd said. *"To let the board cool,"* she'd added. A damn welcome idea after the better part of a year spent soul-bound inside a taxidermied gopher, and on the extreme run from enemies holy and infernal. Upside was he'd quit smoking, downside being the Chief wasn't exactly equipped for Transatlantic travel. Sol felt naked without the old Winnebago parked nearby, rusting away in the gloom of Northern Kent. The kind of uneasy that made him crave a pack of darts like a motherfucker.

"What exactly did Yuvrani tell you?" Sol asked, reaching into his pocket for more peanuts.

"That you've dealt with his sort before," she said. "Daniel asked me to invest in his business, all my savings, plus cash against my pension, even my Nan's pearls. Said I'd get it all back and more. As soon as he got his hands on—"

"A pot of gold?"

"Well," Lydia flushed. "When you put it that way…and even after I caught him rogering Charlotte, the assistant children's librarian he somehow convinced me. He took everything, and then he vanished."

Trace sighed. "Lydia, no."

Lydia clutched Trace's hands. "Have you never been in love, Miss?"

Trace shrugged.

"Hey," said Sol.

Lydia eyed him and then Trace. "Would you not do anything for him? If he asked it of you?"

Trace smirked. "Usually it's me asking for the pearl necklace."

It was Sol's turn to blush as he rubbed a hand over his stubbled scalp. "Did Yuvrani mention we don't work for free? Sounds like you're broke as hell, lady."

Lydia took a breath and composed herself. "Have you heard of *Ghayat Al-Hakim*?"

Trace's eyes flashed. "The *Picatrix*?"

"Arabic text of arcane astrological divination and spells of," she pulled a face, "notable foulness."

"Fuck me," Trace murmured, vibrating in her cheap plastic chair. "An original?"

"In the Gravesend public library?" Lydia gave her a withering look. "No, but we recently acquired a fourteenth century reproduction on vellum. It's authentic."

"On whose authority?" Trace asked.

"On mine," Lydia snapped, stuffing her hankie back up her sleeve. "I'm head of rare books, and if it were only about the money, I'd nick it myself. But that bloody wee bastard ought not be allowed to do to any other woman what he's done to me, not even that tart Charlotte. It's not decent. Bring me that wandering todger of his and the book is yours."

Sol flinched.

Trace tented her fingers. "You want us to track down this leprechaun and cut off his…"

"Will you do it or no?" Lydia said, the chill in her voice giving Sol goosebumps. A fool for love, no doubt, but this librarian wouldn't be fooled twice.

They exited the library onto Windmill Street and made their way down the charming pedestrian thoroughfare. Like walking through a damn theme park and Sol was hit with another fierce craving for his beloved Marlboro Reds. Trace linked her arm through his. "Lydia said he picks up his mail a couple times a week at the post office. We should start there. Gods, this town is a lot."

"I noticed."

"So…traditional."

"Gives me the creeps," Sol agreed as they passed a legit thatched roof cottage on stilts that seemed anachronistic even in a quaint English village. "We're on vacation, and you want to take up a side hustle gunning for deadbeat boyfriends?"

"Leprechaun boyfriends." Trace opened the map on her phone and googled the post office. "How is that not exactly in our wheelhouse?"

"He's not a damn leprechaun. There's no verified evidence they exist, especially not ones that look like they just stepped out of a cereal box. The Church—"

"Okay, Scully." Trace retorted. "I know it's hard to wrap your narrow Catholic brain around anything not in the Bible, but there are other critters out there, and maybe they're still alive because they didn't go around showing off. Ever think of that?"

"He's a grifter, and she's an easy mark. Look at this place, it's practically feudal. He tells her a few fairy tales, bends her over a bookshelf, cleans out her bank account, and now she wants his dick in a box? We're not seriously doing this."

Trace dug around in her bag, pulled out a tattered notebook, and shoved it in his face, opened to a page with a list of titles all crossed out. All but one. *Picatrix*. "I want that book, Sol. And I'd cut *your* dick off to get it. So, let's go."

Christ, he wanted a cigarette. "Let's stop at that kebab place first."

"You just ate." Trace nudged his belly. "Much as I love a dad bod, you might wanna try the gum before you pop out of those Hawaiian shirts you love so much."

"The fatter you are the better they look."

"Like cigarettes are gonna be what kills you?" she sighed, pulling him into the street and away from the strange house on stilts that she kept glancing back at in a way she probably thought he didn't notice.

They located the tiny post office where a slender lad with purple hair and extravagant false eye lashes was pasting a shipping label on a large box for another customer. His name tag read Billy.

"On second thought let's get those kebabs and regroup," Trace said suddenly, grabbing Sol's arm and trying to drag him out the door.

"Wait, what?" Sol said.

"Leaving so soon?" Billy called out in a smoky Russian accent.

Trace froze.

"How may I help you, Lady Black."

Sol growled. "Seriously, does everyone here know who we are?"

Trace approached Billy with a hard unblinking expression. "I guess word travels fast."

"Matushka maybe mention you come see me. Little red fox and her big bad wolf." Billy gave Sol a slow onceover, his glossy lips curved in a smile. "I happen to know they don't grow anything this tall, bald, and handsome local. American?"

"Canadian," Trace cut in. "But we're hoping to find a certain local."

"We just want to talk to him," said Sol.

"You look more like man of action," Billy turned to Trace. "Lisichka, where in the worlds did you find such beautiful brute?"

Trace hoisted her bag on her shoulder. "At Church, believe it or not."

"Praise Jesus," said Billy.

"Short guy," Sol said, impatient and feeling like the butt of a joke everyone but him was in on. "Red hair, wears a lot of green, goes by the name of Daniel—"

Billy tossed his head back in a full-throated cackle. "Donkey Dick Dan?"

Trace's eyes widened. "Guess we know why Lydia wants it back."

"Right, yes," Billy said. "He is legend among ladies of Gravesend. He is opposite to this," he flicked a hand at Sol. "He dress very fine, and rumour is his posh little trousers need special tailor. If you see him, you tell him Billy say hello."

"You and everyone else, it seems. So, where does he live?" Sol asked, leaning on the counter.

"Patience, I get to it." Billy lightly scraped his pink fingernails along Sol's forearm. "Gravesend is post town for hundred wide bits in the lane. This is England after all, more villages than fleas on a sheep."

"Which one then?"

"You are charming, but I am sworn custodian of Royal Mail."

"You're Russian," said Sol.

"Gods, Sol. Don't be so xenophobic." Trace nudged him out of the way. "Billy, I think we can help each other."

"How's that?"

She lunged across the counter, grabbing the back of Billy's hair and mashing his face to the counter while plucking a pair of scissors off the desk, opening the blades and straddling them neatly around the left side of his open mouth. "Way I figure, Dan's mail has gotta be pilling up."

Billy gurgled around the blade, his fan-lashed eyes pleading with Sol.

"So, let us play postie for the day," she said, and then cocked her head at Sol. "And I'll throw in fifteen minutes with the big guy."

"What?" Sol said.

"Wha?" said Billy.

"Or," she squeezed the blades slightly. "I widen that pretty smile of yours." Billy shrieked and a stream of blood trickled from his mouth. "You've always been a vain little shit, but hey, your mouth, your choice."

"What the fuck, Trace?" Sol backed up into a spinning rack of post cards. "You know him?"

"It's been a long time," Trace said, then turned back to Billy. "Look, baby brother. You don't want to get between me and what I came here to do. No one does." She looked up at Sol again. "So, what's it gonna be?"

Indeed what? They'd done worse things for worse people for far less. Usually it wasn't Sol doing those things, but if Trace wanted that book so badly, he'd take a Russian blowjob for the team and ask questions later. A lot of questions.

"Okay," he said stepping up to the counter "Yeah. Fifteen minutes."

Billy began to laugh and Trace smiled, removing the scissors. "Was that so hard?"

"Nice to see you not having changed," Billy said, spitting blood into the trash can behind the desk. He turned his gory grin on Sol. "You, I like very much...for sly sister." He retrieved a plastic bin from under the counter, stacked to the brim with envelopes and packages. "Village called Dode. I never go because it barely exists. Wiped out by plague in the 14th century. There you will find him."

"We're going leprechaun hunting!" Trace shoved the bin into Sol's arms, then took Billy's face between her hands and kissed his bleeding mouth. "Thank you, Vasili."

"Hurry, Lisichka." Billy batted his eyelashes. "White, red, and black, the riders three shall pass. And then she will appear."

Sol hefted the bin in his arms as they exited the post office and turned back onto Bath Street. "What the hell was that all about? Three riders? Who's she? You have a brother?"

"Old hag's tale, a Russian thing." Trace lit a cigarette and Sol steeled his will as she sucked it half-way to the filter in a single ferocious drag. "And he's my foster brother. I've got a few. They turn up from time to time, like cursed pennies."

"And do you always skip the hug and go straight to mutilation?" He wiped a smear of blood from her chin.

She flicked her butt into the pristine Gravesend gutter. "Family is complicated, Sol."

Best to watch where he planted his size twelves as he skirted the quicksand of Things Trace Doesn't Talk About. After all these years, he knew almost nothing about where she came from, though he wasn't surprised to learn she'd spent time in the system. People like Trace weren't often the product of stable loving homes. But he couldn't let everything go; this whole vacation was hinky. Trace insisting they come exactly to Gravesend, and stay with Yuvrani, whom she must have known would blab their presence to anyone who would listen, and just happening to have a job land in their laps, and running into Trace's surprise brother in the post office? There were two things Sol didn't believe in: coincidences, and leprechauns. There seemed to be an awful lot of both in this town, and one way or another he was getting to the bottom of it.

Church bells rung in the noon hour and Sol's stomach grumbled. Trace slipped on her sunglasses, heading south toward the sanctuary of the gurdwara and Sol tugged her arm. "One more stop before we head back to Yuvrani's. Something I saw in the guidebook. Something cool."

"Guidebook?" Trace lowered her shades down her nose. "You sound like a fucking tourist."

"We are fucking tourists. Come on." He stomped down the sidewalk, his flapping orange hibiscus shirt drawing stares from the locals, until they stopped in front a statue. "Check this out. Pocahontas!"

The bronze statue towered atop a stone base. A regal lady, far from her home and her people.

"Okay, possibly cool," said Trace, running her fingers over the engraved stone. "Married so young."

"And what about us?" smirked Sol. "Lady Black has a certain ring to it. Want to get hitched?" He tucked the bin under one arm and slipped the other around her shoulders. "Here in the beautiful English countryside? I can pick up an official Lordship in Scotland for fifty bucks."

She tapped out another Sterling, eyeing a stand of trees lining the street a block up. "You believe in signs?"

He flicked his four-leaf clover zippo as she leaned in for a light, then he pushed his face into the twisted mass of her hair, tasting the sweet miasma of horrible English cigarettes. Christ, he needed something, or someone, to do with his mouth. "Why shouldn't we get married?"

Trace tipped her face up for a kiss, her smoky mouth whispering into his. "You don't go buying a cow when all you want is a steak."

Sol couldn't say he understood her metaphor. Why would she assume all he wanted was meat? Or maybe that was all she wanted? He couldn't speak to the deep and abiding emotional bonds between cows, but for Solomon Black, Trace was endgame, and he slept better not questioning that, or her.

"Let's hit that kebab place." She skipped ahead, detouring around every patch of foliage and muttered something about not fooling anyone when they passed yet another cottage on stilts, identical to the last one.

"This town prepping for a flood?" Sol mused.

Trace towed him along him past the house. "We aren't the only ones in Gravesend that don't belong."

Always something. He'd seen a load of supernatural shit over the years, but the creatures prowling the night around here were more of the soccer hooligan variety, so he wasn't too worried. The greasy stink of a fry up had his stomach rumbling and took his mind off the conspiracy he felt unfolding around him. "I'd murder for a few kebabs right now."

"I can't tell if you're joking," she said, laughing anyway.

Once they'd finished stuffing themselves at Rainbow Takeaway, they returned to Brandon Street. The temple wasn't much to look at from the outside. A narrow building snuggled amidst non-descript three story row houses. If it weren't for the blue sign displaying *Shri Guru Ravidass Gurdwara*, you'd easily mistake it for just another house. Yuvrani met them at the black iron gate set in the chest-high plaster fence, a grin splitting her round face.

"Friends! How are you enjoying your first morning in Gravesend?"

"Like you don't already know," mumbled Sol, dropping the bin of mail to the painted grey sidewalk.

Trace elbowed him in the ribs. "When I remembered your open invitation to visit, I didn't think it would be so fortuitous."

"I thought it'd be a vacation," said Sol, wishing, for the millionth time, he hadn't given up smoking.

Trace ignored him. "We got lucky. A *Picatrix*, I still can't believe it."

"Oh Trace, there is no luck or chance. It's fate. Destiny. You were meant to be here through your own actions, and you are meant to help poor Lydia. In your own...particular fashion."

"Speaking of particular fashion," Trace said and paused a long moment. "How long has that Russian queen been at the post office?"

Yuvrani eyed the bin of letters and parcels. "I do what I can to make all immigrants feel welcome. Unfortunately, it was Billy who introduced Lydia to that scoundrel."

"Hmm, she's kinda bloodthirsty, for a librarian."

"A kindred spirit. I knew you'd get on."

Trace glanced briefly over both shoulders. "Got a car we can borrow? We gotta get to Dode."

Yuvrani stepped back, tugging at the folds of her voluminous Bana. "Fate would not drag you there. Dode is a cursed place. Shunned by the living, and haunted by darkness."

"Jesus," said Sol. He watched Trace light up another Sterling and leaned an arm against the fence, careful to avoid the iron barbs topping the plaster. "Let's go to England, she said. Hit the pubs. Have a relaxing non-adventurous vacation. It'll be fun, she said."

"As opposed to what? Hiding out in Moose Jaw?"

"Well, nothing ever happens there, so it would actually be a fucking vacation."

"You'd be dead of boredom in twenty minutes."

"There's an Arby's."

Trace blew smoke in his face. "We arm wrestled for this and you lost, remember?"

"You bit me."

"Fair and square."

A set of keys flew through the air and Sol snagged them with a quick hand.

"Do not fuck up my car," said Yuvrani as she retreated to the doorway of the Gurdwara, "I will have my Jawak bring up your bags. Vahiguru and very good luc... best wishes."

Sol jingled the keys, hit the fob button, and saw lights flash on a white fiat Panda "Oh, fuck me."

Punjabi top 40 poured from the plastic speakers as they made their way down the back roads because apparently that was the only way to get to some pit of an abandoned village in the countryside. The toy car bounced through ruts and puddles and narrowly avoided the ditches on either side of the approximately three-foot-wide lane, no small accomplishment with Sol's elbows jammed between the window and the gear shift and his knees bent up by his ears. Ears filled with jangling sitar power chords and throbbing bass.

Trace cracked the window until her hair swirled like a storm as she peered out the rear, for the fourth time in as many minutes. "Want me to drive?"

"No."

"Passenger seat goes way back."

"I said no."

"You look like an angry pretzel."

"And you don't have your international driver's license."

"Neither the fuck do you."

"I'm a better left-hand driver.

"You're so full of shit." She reached for the radio dial.

"Don't," he snapped. "I like it."

She pulled up the map on her phone. "This should turn into Wrangling Lane in a few minutes. Isn't much village, so keep your eyes peeled."

"Can't see shit in this fog—hey?" he said as she reached over, running her hands over his hip and under his second favourite Hawaiian shirt. "I like car sex as much as the next guy, but I can barely move here, let alone—"

"Aha," she said, removing his butterfly knife from his pants pocket.

"I didn't say it wasn't worth trying," Sol said, swerving around an apocalyptic pothole.

Trace crawled halfway into the back to rummage through the bin of letters and packages. "I'm gonna open some mail, see what kind of lucky charms fall out."

"Cause why not commit a federal crime in every country?" he muttered, wincing at the sound of Japanese steel sawing into fucking cardboard. "What's behind door number one?"

"A clashing carpet and drapes scheme. Four boxes of Miss Clairol in Red Fox. Didn't see that coming."

"Told you there's no such thing as leprechauns."

Her sweet tartan clad ass nudged his cheek as she continued rummaging. "Billy was right. A lot of junk. Real estate flyers, nutritional supplement catalogues, couple issues of GQ. And what looks like corporate mail from…Triple D Investments."

"Triple D?"

"Y'know, leprechauns can't lie. He must have an incredible tool of persuasion to get all those cougars to hand over their family jewels."

Sol had to laugh. "You don't care about that book. You're just out here to catch some giant green dick."

"Their dicks aren't green—" she squealed as Sol turned his head and bit her rump.

"What's that, Lady Black?" he said into her skirt as she squirmed and he ran his hand up her inner thigh.

"Sol, stop."

"In a minute."

"Fucking stop!" she shrieked, and he saw the shadow through the windshield as Trace kicked back, hooking her boot in the wheel and wrenching hard. Their white ride tottered into the ditch, tipping over on its side with a gentle thud.

"Fuck me with a chainsaw," she growled, elbowing Sol in the neck as she clambered out of his lap. "Yuvrani's gonna be pissed. I told you I should drive." She kicked the door open and climbed out onto the road.

"Trace, wait a goddamn second—"

"Got a death wish, you dumb tit?" she screamed at the blurry figure in the middle of the lane.

Sol unfolded himself from the car and pried open the boot enough to grab hold of what turned out to be a tire iron. Better than nothing. Not much better, but it wasn't like he could smuggle his Glock across the pond. He hiked out of the ditch, slipping in the mud, to find Trace squaring off with a man in a smartly tailored pinstripe suit, a silver tipped cane, and a gimlet glint in his eye that cut through the fog. Sol clocked him at roughly four feet tall.

"Laird and Lady Black, I presume."

Sol cursed under his breath. Did absolutely everyone in this blasted country know who they were?

The dapper little gent swept his fedora off copper curls going brown near the scalp. "Daniel David Darby at your service."

Trace kicked a pebble into a nearby puddle. "You're Donkey Dick Dan?"

The man gave her a cocky grin. "Aye, bit o' town gossip, though I dinna dispute its veracity."

"Town gossip is you're a con man, Dan," said Sol, standing at Trace's side. "One particular librarian took it personal, you rinsing her for every penny."

"Investing," Dan sniffed. "I've a knack for growing the wealth of those who believe. Call it luck. Call it centuries of market trend research. I offered Lydia her own pot of gold and she offered the pleasures of her flesh. She's the one lying if she claims any different."

"And Charlotte?" Trace said, digging a speck of dirt from underneath her fingernail with Sol's knife. "Lydia took issue with you flicking through another librarian's card catalogue."

"Call me a cad, but you seem the sort of lass who understands the difference between love and fidelity. You too laddie, though ye have the constipated hint of a traditionalist. Catholic I expect."

"I'm no more Catholic than you are a leprechaun," said Sol. "From the sounds of it you're not even Irish."

"Shows how much ye know. But unlike you, I cannot tell a lie, not even to myself."

"Then why's a Scottish Leprechaun hiding in the back of beyond with his roots showing?" said Trace.

Dan reflexively touched his clownish hair. "You've got a rather valuable bit o' my property."

"You nearly ran us off the road for box dye?"

"An envelope, with a map inside."

"To the end of the rainbow?"

Dan smirked. "Never touch your own pot, lassie. Number one rule of capitalist growth. You two ought to consider your retirement strategy." He eyed Sol. "Especially at your age."

"Can we dismember him already?" Sol said to Trace.

She held up a staying hand. "What kind of map?"

"The kind dearly purchased, leading to a cache of three-hundred-year-old Dutch Water Board bearer bonds. In addition to paying dividends so long as the Netherlands is inclined to stay above water, they are quite the collector's item. I admit to unforeseen delays, but I now have a buyer, as well as another investor much more terrifying than Lydia. I believe you're acquainted with the Russian postal worker."

"Billy?"

"Aye, Billy's..." he gave Trace a knowing look, "superior, and I'll no be talking about the Royal Mail. In fact, I'm expecting her momentarily."

"Shit," said Trace, glancing around.

"Are all leprechauns as trusting as you?" Sol asked.

Dan nodded. "Trust is an abstraction. This is business. Give me the map, I assure ye it's quite useless in your human hands, and in exchange for graciously allowing me to crack on, I'll see ye well taken care of. Consider it a gratuity, for hand delivering the post."

"Cool story," Sol said. "But we invented this move and we're not falling for it. Are we, Trace?" he glanced over her shoulder and let out an exasperated sigh when she was already scrambling back into the ditch.

"I want to see this map," she said, digging around in the car.

The fog had begun to burn off and Sol was able to see across the road into a verdant green field where there stood an old church and adjacent graveyard. Mist curled around crumbled remains of stone walls and monuments. The sweet scent of grass, rainwater and fertile earth expanded in Sol's head, blotting out all his other senses. A shaft of sunlight speared through the clouds, igniting the vapour in a kaleidoscope of rainbows. So, this was Dode.

He hadn't expected it to be so… he took a few steps to the other side of the road, spotting something. Not a shadow, not darkness at all, the opposite, a flicker of light flitting in and around the gravestones. He took another step.

"Earth to Solomon," Trace said.

"Is that a…a girl?" He could swear he saw pale hair and eyes.

"Tis a magical place, with a tragic history," said Dan. "When the black death swept through, legend has it the sole survivor, a young girl, hid herself away in the church, praying to her Papist god to save her, or perhaps to take her quick. Some say the Dodechild haunts the grounds still."

"I don't see anything—hey!" Trace shouted as Dan yoinked the envelope from her hand and ran, faster than a four-foot man ought to be able, leprechaun or not, straight into the dew drenched field.

Sol turned to Trace, shaking blood from a paper cut across her palm.

"Goddamnit," she muttered. "At least he's headed where we need to go."

"What?" Sol asked, though his voice seemed like it was coming from somewhere else, from someone else.

"She's a greedy little fox, keeping secrets, running from her debts."

"Huh?" he whispered, feeling himself listing side to side in time with an invisible song only the grass could hear.

"Cross that threshold at your peril, wolf. I'm not the only one waiting..."

"Sol!"

He jolted as Trace rapped his forehead with her knuckles.

"I've been screaming at you," she said. "Jesus, do you have a concussion or something?"

"Well, I didn't, until now." He rubbed his forehead.

She pulled his head down examining his pupils. "How about instead of standing there scratching your balls with a tire iron, we go after that fake ginger fucker?"

Sol peered across the field. Trace was lying. Or hiding. Something. Something about this wasn't right. But something else absolutely was. The song rang in his memory. "He's gone for the church."

"And so are we, come on."

"Did I ever tell you I played football in Seminary?" Sol squared off, braced himself, and let fly with all his strength. The iron spun lazily through the air to hit Dan's head with an echoing crack, sending him stumbling right through the stone archway into the church.

Trace dashed a few yards before stopping. "Come on already."

Sol trotted after her, surprised he'd hit Dan. Traditionally his throw was more power than precision, lucky to hit the broad side of a barn. Everything at this moment felt askew, a few degrees off.

"Speedy little bastard." Trace reached the door, partially ajar, a medieval monster of braced oak complete with surrounding creepers, and its own shingled rooflet.

She peeked in. "Only one door, so this shouldn't be hard. Ready?"

"Clever fox…I taught her well."

The same voice from before slithered through his mind, both far away and lover intimate. Had he hit his head when the car rolled? He burped up a bit of kebab breath and realized how hungry he was.

"Let's get this done." And get back to his vacation. Screw saving a few bucks to bunk in Yuvrani's storage closet. Once they got back to town, he'd find a room over a shitty pub and drink and smoke until they got tossed out of the country.

"You'll never make it back to town…"

Trace grabbed his hand, and the sticky heat of her blood smeared his palm. He caught the scent of steel and silver. Saw the auric residue from a hastily cast incantation. Before he could ask what she'd done, she dragged him through the door, under an archway of carved shadow.

And into the light.

Sol had visited many churches in his days. Churches like this tended to be a single room or two, walls adorned with tapestries and narrow stained-glass windows. Ceiling vaulted in wood beams. Worn wooden pews on worn hardwood floors. Crosses. Candles. This though. He spun around, and where the door had been…

"Goddamnit, in and out, that was the deal." Trace smashed her fist against a glossy white wall leaving a crimson smear. She stood back, examining her hand. "The blood…I should have known."

They stood within four walls, white marble shot with silver threads, and a roof open to a bluebird sky. No pews, only piles of assorted cushions, and a dominating gold altar.

"Uh, where the hell are we?" asked Sol.

"Duh, the Summer Court." A teenage elf emerged from behind the altar, garlands of flowers looped over her wrists. "Best place for a party, more... frolicky. And way better food. Winter court is all blood pudding and mulled sheep's milk. Barf."

"Where the hell is Dan?" snapped Trace, yanking a leather folio from her bag and leafing through it.

"Mister Darby? He's around, never misses an all-you-can-eat in the Summer Court, and tonight is gonna be a rager." The girl approached Sol and pressed a string of marigolds into hand. "Get this on." She tossed one woven from vervain to Trace. "You too."

Sol held the garland to his face. Smelled like marigolds, and the girl. At least a girl who washed her hair with lavender and wore Doc Martins, ripped black jeans, and a vintage Def Leppard t-shirt. Had to be a head injury. His mind was a muddle, the last clear thing he remembered was the car hitting the ditch. This felt like oxycodone, and after the last few years of near terminal abuse, he knew his oxycodone. "So, you're the Dodechild."

"I'm a lotta things."

"But you're no ghost. No, this has gotta be Faerie."

"You're smarter than they said you'd be."

"Hardly," muttered Trace, face deep in her book.

The girl curtsied. "I'm Estrid, but call me Sid. I'm supposed to show you to your rooms and stuff. You can chill out in the hot tub before you get into your party clothes. We should get going, you wouldn't believe how time flies around here."

Red flags pushed up like bloody daisies, but whatever the hell was going on, it all felt strangely relaxing. Probably more than they could afford though. "Look… Sid, and I love the shirt by the way. Just how much is this going to cost us?"

"It's covered," said Sid, nodding at Trace. "So, don't worry your regal head. Full service and all inclusive, for… well, forever." She held out a pale hand capped with black fingernails. "Make yourselves at home Lord and Lady Black."

Sol chuckled. "We're not married, kid."

Trace slapped her bloody hand against the wall again. "Nobody is making themselves at home, okay?" She tossed the garland to floor. "I don't know what your game is, you baby faerie bitch, but I'm going to find Dan, and then Sol and I are getting the hells out of here. I'm getting those water board bonds, I'm getting the *Picatrix* from Lydia, I'm getting that Russian Hag off my back and then I'm putting us up over the poshest pup in London. In the meantime," she pointed to Sol. "Don't move, I'll be right back."

"Your lady is a greedy one," Sid remarked after Trace disappeared down a hallway behind the altar.

"Ravenous," Sol agreed.

"I like her."

"So do I," he said, then took Sid's warm hand. "You said hot tub?"

Sid led him into a corridor off the main chapel and into a room with an enormous white bed and crystal vases full of plump white flowers. Emerald green moss grew on slate floor and stone walls. A fire crackled merrily in the hearth.

"What's your favourite record?" Sid asked.

Sol glanced down, again noting her Pyromania t-shirt. "You're wearing it, kid."

"Knew you'd say that!" She grinned and pulled a bottle of Blanton's from an oaken cabinet, pouring several fingers into a crystal tumbler.

He couldn't help noting the stopper was the coveted N with the attached apostrophe. "You seem to know a lot about me."

"Put this on." She held out both the whiskey and a fluffy white robe. "Just until your feast rig arrives. We've been expecting you for some time, but had to make alterations...based on more recent measurements."

Sol took a slug of good bourbon and started unbuttoning his shirt. Sid stood in front of him, wide eyed and eager, silver hair tucked behind her ears. "You mind?"

"Oh!" She spun around. "I envy your culture of privacy. Everyone is up everyone's butt here. It's suffocating. Sometimes I want to run away so badly I could just scream."

"Why would you want to leave," Sol said, shrugging into the robe and nearly groaning out loud for how soft it was. Like wearing a cloud. "This place seems great."

"Is Def Leppard still touring?"

"They aren't what they were, kid. Sorry to say."

"I just want to see them. I want to taste the air full of human electricity on my lips and breathe in the flesh and the sweat and the lights and be invisible in a dark mob. To disappear into the music."

"How do you even know about all that?"

Sid turned around. "Mister Darby got me an iPhone."

"No shit."

"Wanna see the baths?"

Sol was settled in a round pool of bubbling rainbow water when Trace burst into the chamber in a white dress threaded with green and gold vines and blooming with pink and mauve blossoms, like a human bouquet wrapped in silk.

"Jesus H. Christ," he said.

"I was attacked," she said, ripping a spray of crocuses from her hair. Her eyes fell on the tumbler of bourbon in his hand and the decimated platter of beef n' cheddar sandwiches by his elbow. "Oh no….no, no, no…"

"Right? Is this place extra or what?" he asked. "Now take off that insane getup, and get your fine ass in here."

"What are you doing!" she shrieked, eyes wild in a way Sol had rarely seen. "I told you… Fucking hell, what have you done?"

"Just doing like you said, waiting."

"Why did you have to quit smoking, for shit sakes?" another cluster of flowers from her hair hit him in the chest. "Jesus, don't you know anything? I told you to stay put, you knuckle-dragging dumbass!"

Sol's hackles rose. "And if I were your little lap dog, maybe I would have. Last time I checked this is supposed to be my vacation, but it was never a vacation, was it? I may not know much, but I know when you're lying to me. And you've been lying since we booked our plane over here. Way I see it, whatever mess we're in is your goddamn fault because you can't help wanting it all and not wanting to pay for any of it—"

He choked on spring water when she jumped in the pool tackling him, her hands around his neck, her dress wrapping him like a living skin, tight and impermeable, dragging him down to the bottom of the pool. Just when he thought he was about to die in Faerie and wondered what that meant, his head broke the surface.

"You stupid son of a bitch," she snarled, her fingers scraping his cheeks as she kissed him hard. Wet silk clinging to them both like a shroud. "You stupid, stupid… We can never leave. Don't you get it?" She kissed him again and again. "We can never leave."

He kissed her back and it occurred to him that Faerie, with its rainbow hot tub, good whiskey, and endless Arby's, might very well be heaven. But no matter where they were, Trace was home. He clawed at the layers of her dress, tore at silver and gold vines, and chewed through flowers until he found the hot wet skin of her.

"Sol," she sighed as he boosted her out of the pool onto the slick stone. She pulled him onto her, into her, her hair in his mouth, her legs tangled with his. Everything he wanted he had. Right here. And he feasted on it.

They lay tangled and panting for a long while. Finally Trace sat up, dress pooling around her in a soggy nest of herbiage.

"You okay, baby?" Sol asked.

"I'm hungry." She grabbed a half-eaten beef n' cheddar and took a huge bite, chewing deliberately.

"What's all this about not being able to leave then?"

"You need to work on your professional development." She swallowed. "If you'd bothered listening, or reading, or even goddamn googling Faerie," she said, taking another bite, and chasing it with a swig of his bourbon. "You'd know if you eat or drink anything they offer, you're fucked. Indentured. They own your ass."

"Oh…"

She demolished what was left of the sandwich. "I'm not leaving you, Solomon Black."

The heavy doors to the baths burst open and Sid entered, followed by two regally tall faeries in green robes, their blood red hair wound up in crowns of antlers. Sol yanked a shred of Trace's dress over his crotch, while Trace made no move to cover herself at all.

"Splendid," the man boomed, his brilliant smile lighting up the room. "Consummation typically follows the feast, but we are not sticklers for formality in the Summer Court, are we darling?" He turned to the other red-haired royal.

"I'd say the feast will be a mere formality in itself," she said, eyeing the platter of food and empty whiskey tumbler. "Well done, Estrid."

"Mama," she mumbled. "It's Sid."

The woman stroked Sid's cheek and plucked at the girl's ratty black concert tee. "Indeed, though decorum can only slide so far and a *Sidhe* princess must wear an appropriate wedding dress."

"What the hell?" Sol said. "You can't make her get married, she's just a kid for Christ's sake."

"Sol," Trace whispered.

"No, I don't care what the culture is or if I'm being xenophobic or racist or whatever. She's like thirteen."

Trace shook her head. "You don't get it."

"This is not happening, not on my watch."

The royals turned to one another bemused. "We assure you, Lord and Lady Black—"

"You people are sick," Sol said. "And we're not married."

"Yes, we are!" Trace snapped. "It's not the kid's wedding, Sol…it's ours."

A beautiful elf minstrel made magic with a lute while her companion sang what sounded to Sol like the sexiest, saddest song every written. He didn't understand a word of it, of course, but the melody made his chest ache and his pants tight. Just like a proper 80's rock ballad. He drained another tumbler of Bourbon.

"So… we're married?"

"Faerie married. Must happened when we crossed the threshold holding hands. Or something. Bloody enchantments."

"So you had no idea?"

Trace stared off into the crowd as though she hadn't heard him, but he knew she damn well had. And that, he supposed, was as much of an answer as he'd get. He squeezed her hand. "Feels kinda right though. Plus, you look sexy hot, babe."

"You look damn fine too, Lord Black," she said, squeezing back, elegant painted nails scoring his callouses. "Tux suits you."

"Don't think you can look bad in bespoke Armani." The suit was perfection, like everything else in this place. "All of this…well, I didn't think it was possible." After the exchange with the King and Queen, Trace had been swarmed again by a gaggle of elven handmaidens and in short order returned to her white silk and flower splendor. Not that Trace made it easy. The handmaidens huddled together several tables over, and Sol counted a few broken noses and black eyes among them. They'd even tamed Trace's hair, straightened and braided with crocuses, it flowed against her back like a foaming black waterfall.

She ran her fingers through a braid, spilling petals across a bare shoulder. "This is an impossible place. We shouldn't be here."

"It's growing on me. And now we're married, we could settle down for good. Pop out a kid."

The look she gave him. Last time they'd discussed kids he'd been attacked by a badger, and this? Same vibe.

He took another gulp from his refilled glass. They'd been seated at a table at one end of an immaculate green meadow, under a natural arch formed by two intergrown trees, in thrones carved from the living oak. Once settled they'd been given anything they asked for. Bourbon and butter tarts for Sol, and for Trace, Japanese gin and Russian cigarettes.

Trace slammed back her Corpse Reviver and lit up. "I'm bored already."

"Bored enough to have a kid?" He said as a little elf in a gauzy red dress wedged herself between them. "That almost sounds criminal."

"Almost—Jesus, Sid," Trace said holding her cigarette out of the way and nudging the girl off her lap. "Personal space much?"

"Can I have a cigarette?" she asked reaching for the pack of Sobranies.

Sol swiped them away. "Hey, what's this song? It's awesome."

"Of course it is, they wrote it for you after I played them your actual favourite Def Lep album, which I know for a fact is *not* Pyromania." Sid pulled out her petal pink phone. "Here, I'll put it on translate."

Plundering the village
Innocents to slay
Babies drowned in buckets
Virgin skin to flay

Marauders born from hell itself
There's nowhere you can hide
They'll set your living flesh on fire
Hammer nails into your eyes

All they want is suffering
They never ask for much
All they want is death and pain
A cigarette to clutch

They'll tear your bloody head off
When the bourbon's got a grip
And screaming comes so easy
When their knives have torn a strip

They'd sell their blackened hearts
For the sauce of the holy grail
There's no escape from winter wolves
Once set upon your trail

All they want is suffering
They never ask for much
All they want is death and pain
A cigarette to clutch

"Wow," Sol said.

"You're right, this place is growing on me," Trace said, chain lighting yet another cigarette from the bottomless pack of smokes while Sol reached for another butter tart.

The music faded and Sid slipped away as Nebulon, King of the Summer Court, waltzed into the middle of the meadow. Scores of elves and other sylvan creatures shushed as one.

"A toast, friends, to the newest additions to our menagerie." The King held up a tall fluted glass of what looked suspiciously like Rosé. "To Lord and Lady Black. They come with a reputation most foul and credentials to match, perfect weapons with which to take our revenge against those pompous fundamentalists within the Seelie Court. Let our friends shiver and enemies quake." The crowd raised glasses and cheered. A hundred eyes, slits of red and black and gold, glimmered in Trace and Sol's direction. "Tomorrow, we set them loose against young Princess Imogene, fairest of fair, kindest of kind, as she makes her pilgrimage to visit her sister in the Argent Mountains. I'm certain our new pets shall return with her skin, to display in the Hall of Grotesques. The newly constructed Black wing, of course. But that is, as they say, a story for many tomorrows, for now, we FEAST!"

King bowed in their direction before disappearing into a raucous crowd.

Trace dug her nails into Sol's arm. "Fuck, I was afraid of this."

"Of being pets?"

"More like attack dogs. We're indentured, stupid. We ate their bloody food, drank their bloody drinks. They own us, body and soul. They've obviously been planning this for some time. They know us, know our rep and skills, want us to smudge out a few of the fairer kin since they can't break their delicate accord. I should have known, dammit."

"I'm nobody's slave." Sol slugged back the rest of his bourbon. "I didn't get out from under the Dirty Bishop's thumb just to be ordered around by some other psychopath. Much as I hate to leave this place."

"Are you listening? We can't. There's no fucking way out, trust me, I know how this works."

"There's gotta be a way, baby. Magic circle?"

Trace tipped her head back and blew smoke into the sweet meadow air. "If I didn't love you so much, Solomon Black, I'd strangle you with your own bow tie."

The music started up again, an upbeat arena rock melody that set Sol's nerves on fire. He watched as white oak tables were assembled, and mass quantities of food and drink appeared atop them. The crowd swooped and began a feeding frenzy the likes Sol had only seen in low end Vegas casinos. One small figure limped to and fro, assembling a crooked tower of pastries like a Dr. Seuss croquembouche. Dan.

"Why don't we ask him?" Sol said. "He can't lie."

Trace squinted into the crowd. "Slippery little bastard. He went to ground earlier, and I couldn't find the hole he'd crawled into. I hate to say it, but you might be on to something." She stood up. "Dan! Get your miserable micro ass over here."

The leprechaun peeked around his wobbling platter of sweets, head wrapped in blood spotted bandages.

"Don't make me ask a second time, you heard the song." Her voice cut through the music.

Everyone stopped. Everyone looked at Dan. Everyone glared at Dan. Dan slumped, then like a condemned man, shuffled over their table.

"Killer party huh?" Trace said, smiling taking his hand. "It's been a slice but we're about ready to Irish exit outta here. Now I know you've got a way and you're gonna take us with you."

"Afraid I canna give ye that, Lass."

"Gosh that's a shame." Trace said pulling Sol's knife from her bodice and jamming it through Dan's hand into the table beneath with a thunk that made Sol wince. An abrupt shriek burst from the Leprechaun as he dumped his platter and a pyramid of tarts avalanched into Sol's lap. His eyes darted around, narrowing on a couple of drunken satyrs stumbling within earshot. When they'd moved on, he cleared his throat and wheezed. "Aye, ye mad she-demon… I may know of a way out of Faerie indeed."

Trace squeezed Sol's shoulder. He felt a surge of energy, the predatory force she radiated before she pounced on some unfortunate prey.

"And?" She leaned over him.

"And what? Ye think I'd help the likes of you? Black-hearted throat slitters? Oh, you'll fit in quite perfect here."

"Come on, Dan." Sol tossed a... mincemeat, or mince something, tart over his shoulder and held Trace back when she lunged again, this time with a butter knife. "We're all friends here."

"Friends?" Dan gasped, sweating and pale. "I know what Lydia wants and what she offered. If I was in your frankly enormous shoes, I'd be performing that Columbian circumcision the second we crossed the veil. So..." Dan picked up a cinnamon bun and took a bite, chewing slowly and deliberately, even as he quivered in pain. "How's about ye make me an offer?"

"How's about I kick your tiny butt so hard you cough up a Louboutin?" said Trace.

"I like the sound of that." The Queen's voice floated over the din as she glided over, wrapped in a sheet of silver gauze that left nothing to the imagination. "Is this rodent bothering you? He is a wretched creature, if generously...endowed." She gave Dan a wink. "But I've grown weary of his antics. So please, destroy him utterly. We build a great fire after dessert, and a live leprechaun burning is an order. Consider it the first of your many tasks." And at that, she strolled away.

"Aw, Dan, you didn't?" Sol grimaced. "The Queen?"

"Like you'd be tossing an arse like that out o' your bed?" Dan gazed after the Queen's indeed tempting backside. Then he wiped his available hand on his emerald vest and tugged his faux-red beard. "As mentioned, I canna tell a lie, and indeed I canna give what ye require. Namely, Fae blood."

"Shouldn't be hard," said Trace, taking hold of the grip on Sol's knife.

Dan flinched. "*Royal* Fae blood."

"It's yours, if you take me with you." Sid said, once again appearing between them. "Hey, Mister Darby."

"Forget it, kid" said Sol.

"Then good luck getting royal blood." Sid flounced in her red dress. "Look, I'm your ride outta here. You want my help or not?"

Trace cursed under her breath.

The large tables clogging the meadow vanished beneath an army of servant types, replaced by smaller ones loaded with silver frosted black cakes topped with perfectly crafted edible versions of Trace and Solomon. In the center of the meadow a twenty-foot circle of grass was pried up to reveal a fire pit where a pyre of logs was assembled and lit.

"We need to go. Now," said Dan, snatching his green cap off his bandaged head and clutching it to his chest. "Princess, might ye conjure a wee glamour that'll obscure our scarpering? Lady Black," he gestured to his impaled hand. "If you please, lass."

With a yank and a yelp, Trace tucked the pack of Sobranies down the front of her dress, handed the bloody knife over to Sol. "Don't suppose we have time to go back to the room and get my bag? I've got a lot of valuable books in there."

Sid shook her head. "Glamour's up. We'll have five minutes, tops. Well of Worlds?"

"Closest and easiest. Follow me." Dan darted around the table and behind the thrones, disappearing into the forest beyond.

Sol grabbed the half empty bottle of Blanton's, another strudel, and took a long look at the closest table of cakes.

"Jesus." Trace grabbed his arm and dragged him into the woods, feet slipping on dew damp grass, every step easier than the last, until they reached a small clearing with a stone well, guarded by an elf soldier in black scale armor and a peaked helm. The soldier had a sword pointed at Dan.

"Sheath your weapon," demanded Sid. "And let us pass."

"Sorry, your highness," rumbled the soldier softly. "The Well is off limits by edict of the King."

"You really want to annoy the King with this? On feast day?"

"Uh, well I—"

A horn blew a long resounding note from the direction they'd come, followed by three short blasts.

"Dammit, we don't have time for this," said Trace.

Sol thrust his handfuls of party booty into Trace's hands, picked up Dan, and swung the leprechaun like a flail at the soldier. Startled, the elf stepped backwards, tripped against the stones ringing the well, and plunged in screaming.

More horns blasted and voices filled the forest.

"Chop, chop," said Trace, grabbing Sid's arm. "Blood?"

"Right." Sid pulled a black needle from her boot, pricked her finger, and applied a drop of crimson to both Trace and Solomon's foreheads. "You'll have to carry me, this has to be an abduction. Best to carry Dan, too. Otherwise who knows where we'll end up."

Trace took hold of a wobbling Dan and Sol scooped up Sid. "So, we jump?"

"Aye, laddie. Close your eyes and think of Scotland."

Sol wasn't rightly sure what he was thinking of, but in the end he did the only thing that mattered. With Sid's skinny arms yoked around his neck and the chunky tread of her combat boots scraping his sides, Sol tried to situate himself mid-freefall for what was sure to be a bad landing no matter which way was up.

"Trace!" he shouted as they fell, endlessly through the dark. "Trace, goddamnit, where are you?"

Sid's hair flew into his mouth when he opened it to scream again, but then he felt a hand clutch his. A hand he'd know anywhere.

"Here," she said. "Right here."

"You got Dan?"

"Um…" She uttered a muffled squeak and her hand tightened around his. "Yeah, I…have him."

"Jesus," he muttered, stomach lurching with regret. Shouldn't have chased those butter tarts with so much bourbon, no matter how smooth it was. "We're gonna die."

"This is the way," Sid said into the back of his neck. "You'll see."

"She's right." Trace laughed, the sound ringing in the void. "Sol, we're not falling. We're flying."

"Aye," Dan spoke up at last. "It'll no be long now."

Sol blinked as a pinpoint of light appeared in the distance, growing larger and larger and he braced for impact when they exploded through the portal and slid across something cold and wet. Sid mashed Sol's face into the muck as she pushed herself to her feet.

"Wicked!" she said. "I can't believe how beautiful it is."

Sol rolled and sat up, dazed, the smell of low tide wafting over him. Trace staggered like a princess dragged through the mud, gathering her wits. Beautiful was not the first word that came to mind. Dirty field stone walls and the ruins of yet another church with a few rotting wooden crosses in the graveyard. The rest was moss and mud, as far as the eye could see, which wasn't very owing to heavy fog. Mostly, it was brown.

"Back so soon..." that strange voice returned, eeling through Sol's own thoughts.

"Welcome to Foulness Island," Dan exclaimed, hands on his tiny hips, hat perfectly perched on his bloody bandages and brassy red curls.

"Foulness..." Sid took a deep blissful breath. "The human world. I can't believe I'm really here."

"Well yer Highness, not exactly," said Dan.

"What do you mean?" Trace said, wiping the mud off her face. "Our deal was we save your ass if you get us home."

"And I'd caution ye not to get yer knickers in a twist, were ye wearing any," Dan said, gracefully dancing back a few steps as Trace advanced. "I promised to get ye out of Faerie, and get ye out, I have."

"You slimy imp."

"Don't you talk that way to Mister Darby!" Sid snarled, stepping between Trace and Dan. Sol knew it was about to get ugly, that he should probably do something, but his boots were sunk to the ankles in mud.

"Listen up, Tinkerbell." Trace squelched over to Sid, cupping her shimmery cheeks in both hands, leaning in until their foreheads touched. "It's a man's world out there, and if a girl wants to survive, she learns real quick to talk to any mister, any way she goddamn well pleases."

Sid's eyes widened, then blinked. "Can I have a cigarette?"

"Sure, honey." Trace reached down the front of her dress.

Sol lurched free of the mud, boots nearly sucking off his feet. "You can't give cigarettes to a kid."

"I've been smoking since I was like two hundred years old."

"Besides, you're not her dad," Trace added, handing the pack to the geriatric teenager. It was all Sol could do not to rip them from her hand

and chain smoke every last one down to the gold leaf filter.

Sol threw up his hands and turned to Dan. "What the hell is this place then?"

"A crossing, lad. The sort to be found if ye know where to look for the old ways between places." He pointed to the shore where brown water lapped up through the fog. "We'd best make haste while the tide is out. It's six long miles to Wakering Stairs where you'll find yourselves back where you belong, for good or ill."

They followed Dan to the shoreline, where they were greeted by a storm-battered sign and the stench of marine rot.

Essex Broomway
Use At Own Risk
Not Responsible For Mud Deaths

A vague path led out to the water.

"I don't like this," Sol said. "Feels like a trap."

"He's a leprechaun," Trace said, lifting the filth crusted skirts of her wedding dress out of the muck. "What's he gonna do, bite our knees off?"

"Way used to be marked with broomsticks and such," Dan called out over his shoulder. "Not so many nowadays but keep yer feet on the high land and all will be well." Sid scampered over the spongey trail while Sol seemed to sink a few inches with every step. Mud deaths, he thought, peering over the endless expanse of black ooze.

"Fool. You choose this, rather than ride out your days in bloody comfort, with your Lady Black?"

They trudged, on and on, through fog, over mud marked occasionally by the weathered remains of a broomstick, slipping and sliding, and occasionally sinking, while Sid and Dan capered effortlessly over the perilous terrain. With every step Sol forced down the rising animal panic in his chest. Riding out his days... Riders three... White car, Red dress... Lady Black.

"I'm sorry," Trace whispered, so softly Sol thought he imagined it.

"Never trust a leprechaun..."

"Did you say something?" he asked but a ferocious roar tore through fog and his bones shook as footsteps approached. The footsteps of something huge. "What the hell?"

"I believe you're well acquainted with our mutual creditor." Dan said.

"Dan, what did you do?" Sol asked.

A house on stilts breached the fog, looming over them, weather-furred boards and black windows forming a wrinkled, scowling face of a wooden hag. The hut stomped closer on what, upon closer scrutiny, weren't stilts at all but giant chicken legs.

Dan shook his head, "I'm afraid she's no happy with ye, Lady Black."

"You sawed off motherfucker," Trace said. "You were working for her the whole time, you set me up."

"Aye, and I thank ye for makin' it dead easy. She knows ye better than ye know yerself. Every crumb she tossed out, a wee leprechaun getting' ye into faerie for a quick jump over the broom. The arcane text, the water board bonds, even when you could've thrown me on the pyre and lived out your days in gory splendour wi' the Fae, ye couldna resist chasing that pot o' gold."

"How did you know we wouldn't kill you?"

Dan shrugged. "I didna, but scairt as I am of fiery death or you excising me manhood, Baba Yaga scares me loads more. Trying to steal your soul back from a Russian witch, lass. Ye ought to know better."

"Baba Yaga?" Sol said. "That's Baba Yaga?"

"Not a great time for questions, Sol," Trace said, closing her eyes and whispering to herself. "Damn it, I need my books."

Sol ignored her "Is that what this is all about? Us coming here? This supposed vacation? You reneged on a deal with Baba Yaga? When did this happen? How?"

The house rose up, front door banging open in a howl reeking of old blood and dead leaves.

"Oh shit...shit...run!" Trace said, breaking into a sprint.

"This is rad!" Sid screamed as they ran. "I know all your stories and songs, but this is blowing my mind. You guys are sooooo cool."

"Yeah, really fucking cool," Sol said. "And really fucking dead, in a minute."

The stomping of those monstrous chicken legs drew ever closer. Sid and Dan ran with inhuman speed and agility, soon disappearing into the fog. Trace stumbled in that goddamn dress, tripping over the trailing vines and shreds of silk and fell flat on her face. Sol skidded to a stop, immediately sinking into the mud, and wrenching himself back.

"I gotcha, baby," he said, hauling her up.

"No, Sol—"

Sol's breath blasted out in a whoosh when a clawed foot lifted from the mud and batted him off the path and into the marsh where the ooze immediately started to swallow him. Jesus, he was going to drown in this shit. He thrashed and tried to half crawl half swim back to the path. Then a long branch of an arm slithered through a side window of the house and plucked him up by the back of his tux, suspending him high above the Broomway. The stitching under his armpits popped from the strain. Armani. A good brand to die in.

"Now you will pay for what you have stolen, wolf."

"Mama!" Trace screamed. "Mama, stop!"

Sol glanced at the ugly house, seeming to sneer through its windows and doors. "Baba Yaga is your fucking mother?"

"Family is complicated," Trace said, shaking with tension and turning her focus back to the house. "Mama, goddamn it, you know it's too late. It was always too late. You need to stop this."

The house wailed, a terrible sound that gloved Sol's heart in ice.

"I know I promised," Trace said. "But I was just a kid, I would have promised you anything."

The house seemed to slump in defeat, and Sol's hopes rose slightly, until he realized the house wasn't surrendering. It was sinking.

"Mama, put him down. We need to get out of here."

The house growled. Sol's left sleeve ripped and he fell a few inches. "Fuck, okay. Nice house. I uh...always wondered where she came from and you...well I can see where she gets a lot of her…personality. It's not a bad thing, I like a woman with a little blood on her hands."

"Sol, shut up," Trace barked and crouched to the ground, digging her fingers like tree roots into the mud, and began whispering.

The house shuddered and screamed as it sunk another ten feet, finally it swung Sol out and hurled him into the fog. He braced himself for a dire mangling when he hit the ground, but he went hydroplaning across the mud and came to an only moderately painful stop, wrapping himself around a broomstick. He rolled over to see the house struggling on its terrible chicken legs to free itself, from the marsh. Trace whispered feverishly, her wet hair whipping around her head from an invisible gale. Sol crawled to her side and was instantly driven back again by the terrible heat radiating off her body. Her tears evaporated into steam the instant they fell but Sol saw them nevertheless.

"I see your end wolf, as you see mine, and they are the same. Lisichka cannot fight her nature."

Sol lay on the relatively stable ground of the Broomway path as Trace sent whatever magic she'd learned in that house into the earth. Foot by foot, she sank. Until finally the chimney disappeared.

Dan hadn't been kidding when he said it was a long way. They'd been walking for hours, maybe a whole day. Sol's stomach growled hideously, but even that was a welcome interruption to the scrape and suck of their feet in the mud. Trace kept her head down, her arms wrapped around herself. She didn't speak. Step after step after step.

"I'm sorry about your mom," Sol finally said.

"Like it was going to end any other way?"

"Tell me," he said. Not a question, not a demand, but an offer. Of space for her to lay out whatever she wanted, in whatever way she needed to.

"She found me," she said. "In an abandoned tenement in one of those eastern bloc countries. She never told me where. I was maybe four years old, living naked and feral, with a family of foxes. *Lisichka,* she called me. Red fox. She raised me, taught me everything. There were others too, a whole litter of wildings, including Vasili. But I was hungry, I needed to leave. I needed the world. She gave me her blessing, on the condition that I return to her one day. And I meant to. I thought I had no choice. But then I met you, you big moose, and you taught me the one thing she didn't."

"Yeah, what's that?"

"That I don't owe anyone my soul."

Sol stopped, and immediately began to sink in the mud. He knew he'd heard it earlier. Heard her say the words. He knew because he'd never, not once, heard her say them before. And now he knew they weren't meant for him, but for someone she loved, before she loved Sol, someone she loved still. But that love didn't stop her. Nothing ever did. She wanted it all. She had secrets. And he could take that, or leave it, for better or worse.

"Jesus, Trace, what a fucking mess. All this Faerie shit – we're still indentured, by the way – you tricked me in to marrying you when all you had to do was ask. Why not just tell me the truth? We could have gone after her together."

"And do what? She's Baba Yaga, I don't have that kind of power."

"But you just…" he gestured to the sea of mud.

"You think that was me?" Trace laughed. "I wasn't trying to sink her, Sol. I was trying to save her."

"What? Why?"

"I keep telling you, family is complicated." She wrung her ruined rag of a dress between her fists, hair flowing like dirty rivers over her wet shoulders "And I didn't tell you the truth because I know what it—what *marriage*—means to you. This wasn't that. It was only about busting the contract, if my soul wasn't entirely mine to give, she wouldn't be able to take it."

"A loophole."

"I couldn't ask you. Not for that."

"Yet here we are."

"Here we are."

"You're a greedy thing," he said, pulling her into his arms, smelling the rank mud in her hair, and feeling the electric hum of old magic under her skin. "You wanting that soul of yours returned, Lady Black?"

She leaned her head against his chest, over his heart. "Ride or die, baby."

"Trace?"

"Sol?"

"We're sinking."

The fog thinned as they reached the shore and Sol couldn't help smiling at the sight of Dan and Sid on the beach, with Yuvrani's Fiat fucking beat to shit Panda.

"Congratulations on a successful crossing, friends," Dan said with a bow.

Sid hopped off the car roof. "We thought you were dead."

"You little fungus," Trace growled and lunged through the sand, bare hands hooked into claws.

Sol grabbed her around the waist, pulling her back just before she could tear Dan's day-glo hair out by the roots. "Let it go, Trace. For Christ's sake."

Dan composed himself, clutching his napkin wrapped hand, though the fear still showed in the whites of his emerald green eyes. "I knew the mud wouldna' take her weight for long. Bigger baddies than Baba Yaga've been swallowed whole by the Black Lands."

Trace wrestled free and managed to clap Dan a good one across the face. Then she took a deep breath and stood down. "My mother is maybe dead because of you."

"Inconvenienced at most." Dan brushed his lapels with care. "And I saved your life, lass. Or at least that of your Laird husband. And after what we shared in the Well of Worlds…"

"Knock it off, you dick dragging creep. I've had better, and don't pretend you did us a favour when all you did was arrange for one less swindled investor wanting your meat on a platter."

"Aye, but you would have done the same. We know that to be true so don't bother arguing the point."

Sol nodded to Trace. "It's a good point."

"So you won't be needing this then?" Sid asked, pulling a 44 magnum out of the folds of her red dress.

"Jesus, fuck—where'd you get that?" Sol asked.

She brushed silver hair out of her eyes. "Glove box."

"Yuvrani had that in her…this whole time I could've been packing—"

"Thanks, honey." Trace swiped the cannon from Sid's hands and aimed it at the visibly sweating leprechaun. "Way I see it, Dan, you did help me. And now with my mom out of the picture, there's still the matter of Lydia's book and those water board bonds. So, I'm thinking you can help me just a little bit more. Sol, get your knife out."

"Are we really doing this?" Sol groaned, pulling out his knife and after a moment's consideration, tucking it down the front of her wedding dress.

"What are you doing?" Trace said.

"Seems like your hands are full."

"Yeah, I can't hold a gun and de-bone a leprechaun at the same time. All I want is a little help."

"All you want is everything." he said, kissing her forehead. "Find me at the pub when you're done here. Come on, kid. Let's get you your first human world pint."

Sid scampered to his side and they strolled down the beach, leaving Trace – Faerie-law wife, daughter of a Russian myth, schemer, grifter, and partner for better or for worse – to sort out her own destiny. A shaft of sunlight broke through the gloom as Sid held out the crumpled pack of Sobranies. Sol tapped one out, flicked his zippo, and lit up.

THE EPICUREANOMICON

CURATED BY
THE PURGATORIO TOWERS TENANT
ASSOCIATION

Ever crave something like a glass of milk and decide that because one glass of milk was so good that many more glasses of milk would be better and you drink all the milk until the milk is gone but the void inside is still shrieking this horrible hungry black wail demanding to be filled and the first thing you see is a jar of mayonnaise and once that's gone you kinda hate yourself but figure being full of milk and mayonnaise isn't so bad as long as it might be considered a proper meal like a sandwich because if you were to die right now and they did an autopsy they would find all the components for a sandwich and a glass of milk which while sure it's like a lot of those things but still a totally normal meal wholesome even and they won't judge you no one will judge you and so you tear into that pack of bologna and grab a fistful of bread.

Vomitus Bacchanalius

YIELD: 1 Vomitus Bacchanalius.

INGREDIENTS
- 100 gallons of lagno (prepared from an extraterrestrial harvest of limko).
- 300 gallons of human vomit.
- Immeasurable supplies of cosmic dread.

PREPARATION
- Mix, serve, and profit!

Death Shot, with a Twist

YIELD: Makes 1 drink.

INGREDIENTS
- 7.25 oz of Pure Liquid Cocaine. If unavailable, 205.53 grams of cocaine mixed with water will do. Note: a larger glass may be needed for any increased volume.
- 0.75 oz of Lime Juice.
- Recreates the foggy uncertainty of dying (metaphorically) in a glass.

TOOLS
- One 8 oz shot glass (10% off and next-day free shipping for Factory Prime members who use <u>this affiliate link</u>).

PREPARATION
- Mix and serve – straight up.

Melon Ball Fizzy Pop Float w/ Helmet

YIELD: Makes 1 drink.

INGREDIENTS
- A melon – watermelon, honeydew or cantaloupe will work.
- Favourite soda.
- Vanilla Ice Cream.

TOOLS
- Melon scoop.
- Large knife.
- Twine.

PREPARATION
- Cut the melon in half.
- Scoop the fruit out in balls and put in bottom of a large glass (or bucket).
- Add a few scoops of ice cream.
- Pour favourite pop.
- Enjoy!

For the added helmet:
- Clean the inside of the rind until it's clean and free of fruit.
- Cut a hole in each end.
- Thread twine through hole and adjust depending on the size of your head.

Dance like no one is watching!

Fresh Tuny Salad

YIELD: Makes 1 salad.

INGREDIENTS

- 10 ounces fresh chunks of Tuny flesh (That is, the flesh of a girl thirteen years of age, sporting the nickname of Tuny, preferably within 2 hours of perishing).
- 4 large splats of mayonnaise.
- 2 massive globs of unsalted, creamed butter.
- 3 ribs of celery, diced.
- 1/4 red onion, finely chopped.
- 1 tablespoon lemon-infused blood from a teenaged girl (preferably one who goes by the name of Petunia, Tunia, or Tuny).
- 6 dill pickles, chopped into small cubes.
- 1 turkey neck, de-fleshed and crushed to dust.
- Salt and pepper to taste.
- 1 loaf of freshly baked sourdough from the corner bakery.

PREPARATION

- Prepare each ingredient accordingly.
- Mix in medium-sized bowl until all flesh is coated, and the mixture turns a creamy pink.
- Slice the fresh-baked bread.
- Spread an ample portion of Tuny salad on a slice of bread and top with a second slice of bread.
- Cut into six squares.
- Present Tuny salad mini-sandwiches on grandma's silver platter.

The perfect pre-dinner appetizer for any family gathering.

Vegan Sushi Roll

YIELD: Limitless, potentially.

INGREDIENTS
- 1 lb Ground vegans (assorted).
- 2 C Sticky sushi rice, cooked.
- 1 Avocado, slivered.
- 1/3 C Radish sprouts.
- 1 pkg Nori, toasted.

PREPARATION
- Spread rice in a layer over one sheet of nori.
- Arrange spicy vegan crumble, avocado, and radish sprouts crosswise in the middle of the sheet.
- Roll, shape, slice, insta, and serve.

#VeganLife #PlantBased #EatClean #Blessed
#MeatIsMurder

King of King's Grease Burger

YIELD: Makes 16 burgers.

INGREDIENTS

- 4 pounds of regular ground meat (any sort, fattier the better).
- 4 Eggs (any sort).
- Worcestershire sauce (lots).
- 1 cup liquified bacon grease.
- Salt (as much possible).
- Ground black pepper.
- Cumin.
- Crushed garlic.
- Cayenne pepper.
- 16 slices pepper jack cheese.
- 48 Pickles.
- Mustard (yellow, if possible).
- Ketchup (red, if possible).
- 16 sawdust buns (thinner the better).

PREPARATION

- Form meat into patties, using egg, liquified bacon grease, and Worcestershire sauce as a binder and add salt, pepper, cumin, garlic, and cayenne pepper to taste.
- Preheat your bbq to 350°F and grill the burgers for 5-7 minutes, flipping halfway through. Once burgers have been flipped, top each patty with a slice of pepper jack cheese and remove from heat once enslimed.
- Prepare bun by applying a liberal amount of Ketchup and three pickles to the bottom half of the bun, and mustard to the top half.
- Place patty in bun, wrap in foil, and let sit.

Eat singly, or by the dozen!

PURGATORIO TOWERS GAZETTE

TENANT ASSOCIATION

Social Committee

Egg Hunt volunteers needed! While there are technically no terrestrial seasons in Purgatory, the radiance of creation is shifting to the scarlet and that, as we all know, means the Spring Equinox is right around the corner! Volunteers will gather ova from the Tenebraen Abyss and, should they survive, hide them in the Garden of the Cenetaph off the back entrance to Terrace I for the younger, prouder, members of our community.

A Celebration of Poetry

Auditions for the Winter Solstice Poetry Slam will be held in the morning lava ponds on Wednesdays until all slots filled. A fabulous opportunity to be noticed and despised. More detail to follow!

Special Announcements

The screaming from beneath the concrete floor of the Basement Commons—which continued at length until mysteriously ceasing and in fact was found never to have been heard at all—has returned. The extroverts are asked to turn up the volume on their video conferencing until further notice.

Roy from Terrace III once again reminds everyone that there are seven categories of recyclable plastic and that each goddamn category has a corresponding goddamn color coded bin assigned to it. He's made it quite clear that the next degenerate he finds putting a red PVC #3 in a yellow PC #7 bin will have their mating arms torn off and fed to Terry on Terrace VI, in a gesture of reconciliation.

Factory Overstock Sale!

BOGO! Miss Clairol: Red Fox semi-permanent hair colour.

Full Gimp Suits. Go a shade darker with the Limited Anish Kapoor Edition.

Measured shot glasses. Know exactly how much cocaine is in your Columbian Jagerbomb.

Memorial Service

Tuny Casserole. Service will feature a closed casket. In lieu of flowers, please consider donating to Terry's Label Printer Crowdfunder

Personals

Charlie from Terrace VII needs new players for his Friday night poker game.

Fight Club in the Purgatory Pub. This week, for three days only, take on the King of Kings.

Old Lady seeks Fly. DM for details.

Buy/Sell/Swap

For sale: Three-hundred-year-old Dutch Water Board bearer bonds. No reasonable offers refused.

Giant bean bag chair, slight rip on the side, super comfy. Not entirely filled with beans. $8

V's Housekeeping. Low rates. Abuse tolerated and in fact encouraged.

Looking for tickets to the Stampede, hear it's weird this year. Willing to pay $$$.

Lost and Found

One Vegan cat (Lazlo). Wretched thing. Won't answer to his name. Found hiding in the East Wailing Shrine. If not claimed will be dropped off at the nearest incineration depot before Terry adopts yet another stupid land mammal.

Funnies

Copyright © 2021 One-Handed Nihilism

ABOUT THE AUTHORS

Mike Thorn ("Vomitus Bacchanalius") is the author of the novel *Shelter for the Damned* and the short story collection *Darkest Hours*. His fiction has appeared in numerous magazines, anthologies and podcasts, including *Vastarien, Dark Moon Digest, The NoSleep Podcast, and Tales to Terrify*. His film criticism has been published in MUBI Notebook, The Film Stage, and In Review Online.

Visit his website mikethornwrites.com or connect with him on Twitter @MikeThornWrites).

Eddie Generous ("Naked Samantha") has fallen off three different roofs and been lit on fire on multiple occasions. He grew up on a farm and later slept with his shoes under his pillows in homeless shelters. He dropped out of high school to afford rent on a room at a crummy boarding house, but eventually graduated from a mediocre college. He is the author of several small press books, has 2.8 rescue cats (one needed a leg amputation), is a podcast host, and lives on the Pacific Coast of Canada.

You can find Eddie online at www.jiffypopandhorror.com

Robin van Eck's ("Fat Apocalypse") stories and personal essays have appeared in various literary magazines and anthologies across Canada and internationally such as *Lamplight, FreeFall, Prairie Journal, Woven Tales Press, Waiting: An Anthology of Essays, Very Much Alive* and more. Her first novel, *Rough,* was published by Stonehouse Publishing in November 2020.

More information at www.robinzvaneck.com

Cam Hayden ("Gluttony") draws strange comics, cartoons, makes odd prints and things like that. A lot of his inspiration comes from underground comic folks and an early exposure to Mad Magazine and National Lampoon. He also makes goofy trading cards.

Find Cam online on Twitter at @Lancegoiter or at www.patreon.com/lancegoiter.

Konn Lavery ("Death Shot") is a Canadian author whose work has been recognized by Edmonton's top five bestseller charts and by reviewers such as Readers' Favorite, and The Wishing Shelf Awards.

He started writing stories at a young age while being homeschooled. After graduating from graphic design college, he began professionally pursuing his writing with his first release, *Reality*. He continues to write in the thriller, horror, and fantasy genres.

He balances his literary work along with his own graphic design and website development business. His visual communication skills have been transcribed into the formatting and artwork found within his publications supporting his fascination of transmedia storytelling.

Find Konn online at www.konnlavery.com.

Julie Hiner ("Tuny") is an author, storyteller, and blogger. She has independently published an inspirational work of non-fiction and two dark crime novels. Two of Julie's short horror stories have been published in anthologies, and she is currently collaborating in the horror realm. Julie's home-base is KillersAndDemons.com where she serves up toxic cocktails of 80s metal, ritualistic murder, and raw horror.

Julie lives in her hometown in Canada, nestled near the Rocky Mountains. A hardcore 80s rocker at heart, Julie's writing is infused with music of all eras. Her dark crime novels are a fusion of 80s metal, 70s acid rock and dark story telling. Obsessed with the dark mind of the serial killer, Julie's characters are based on bits and pieces of some of the most terrifying monsters to roam the earth.

Find Julie online at killersanddemons.com.

Sarah L. Johnson (curator) is a curly hair gladiator, ultramarathoner, literary events wrangler, and misfit fictioneer. Her stories have appeared in *Vastarien, Room Magazine, Plenitude, On Spec, Shock Totem, Crossed Genres, Year's Best Hardcore Horror Vol. 2* (Red Room Press), and the Bram Stoker Award nominated *Dark Visions 1* (Grey Matter Press) and *Twisted Book of Shadows* (Haverhill Press). She's the author of *Suicide Stitch: Eleven Tales* (EMP Publishing) and co-author of *Terrace VII: Wall of Fire* (The Seventh Terrace).

Find Sarah on Twitter @leadlinedalias or at www.the-seventh-terrace.com

Robert Bose (curator) has a fondness for cosmic horror, sword and sorcery, pulp adventure, and Bourbon, not necessarily in that order. He's the editor and co-publisher of various crime, pulp, and horror books and anthologies - formerly for Coffin Hop Press and currently for The Seventh Terrace. He's the author of various stories and books including the collections, *Fishing with the Devil* and *Terrace VII: Wall of Fire* (with Sarah L. Johnson). When not writing, editing, publishing, reading, and running ultramarathons, he spends his time annoying his wife, pestering his troublesome children, and working as a Chief Architect for an economic forecasting software company.

Find Robert on Twitter @RobBose, on FB at www.facebook.com/robertbose, or at his website at www.robertbose.com.

The Seventh Terrace

Visit us online at
www.the-seventh-terrace.com

ALSO AVAILABLE FROM THE SEVENTH TERRACE

Unfortunate Elements of My Anatomy

The Walking Son

Starseed

End of the Loop

Trace & Solomon: Torrington

Terrace VII: Wall of Fire

The Black City Beneath

Infractus

Fishing with the Devil

Futility: Orange Planet Horror